Y0-BXI-286
The University Library
UNIVERSITY OF CALIFORNIA/RIVERSIDE

GAMBUSINO

PLOVER CONTEMPORARY LATIN-AMERICAN CLASSICS IN ENGLISH TRANSLATION SERIES

Notes of a Villager by José Rubén Romero
Calling All Heroes by Paco Ignacio Taibo II
Qwert and the Wedding Gown by Matías Montes Huidobro
Gray Skies Tomorrow by Silvia Molina
Blood Relations by Carlos Montemayor
Gambusino by Carlos Montemayor

GAMBUSINO

A NOVEL BY

CARLOS MONTEMAYOR

TRANSLATED BY

JOHN COPELAND

Plover Press
Kaneohe, Hawaii
1997

For information, address the publisher,
Plover Press, POB 1637, Kaneohe, Hawaii 96744

Printed and Bound in the United States of America

Cover illustration: "Lobo Aullando en la Luna" by Rufino Tamayo,
courtesy of the Honolulu Academy of Arts, gift of Robert Allerton

Library of Congress Cataloging-in-Publication Data

Montemayor, Carlos, 1947–
[Minas del retorno. English]
Gambusino / by Carlos Montemayor ; translated by John Copeland.
p. cm. — (Plover contemporary Latin-American classics in
English translation series)
ISBN 0-917635-21-3 (cloth : alk. paper). — ISBN 0-917635-24-8
(pbk. : alk. paper)
I. Copeland, John, 1930– . II. Title. III. Series.
PQ7298.23.0688M513 1997
863—dc21 96-53996
CIP

Distributed by Academy Chicago Publishers
363 West Erie Street
Chicago, IL 60610

Translator's Preface

Gambusino sold 31,000 copies in Mexico, where it won first prize in *El Nacional*'s fiftieth anniversary novel contest. Its success was owing in part to its unparalleled richness of style, an evocation of the psychological through the natural, especially as it relates to the hero, Alfredo Montenegro's, state of mind. Never perhaps in the history of Mexican literature has a drinking scene in a brothel been so believably detailed as it is in *The Present V*, or in *The Present VIII* the death of a man. *Gambusino* is a story in the purest sense of the word and therefore can be read without a thought to its historic context, just as a child enjoys the beauty of the day outside a window where dislocation, famine, and death might be going on. These are in *Gambusino*, and the Mexican reader who is not aware of them hardly exists. When Pancho Villa, an illiterate man, was asked if he could speak English, he answered, "Sí, American Smelting and Refining y sonofabitch."

The implicit background begins with the assassination of Francisco I. Madero, an "Anti-Reelectionist" and father of Mexico's tradition of peaceful accession. By legal means he would have dissolved the large land holdings and ended the cavalier way in which his country's natural resources were being made available to foreign powers. Instead, the U.S. Ambassador, Henry Lane Wilson, sided with Madero's assassin, Victoriano Huerta. Wilson, a Taft appointee and no friend of the man who later became president, was committed to American business interests in Mexico generally, and more specifically to those of the American Smelting and Refining Company, which belonged to the Guggenheim family. When the author of *Gambusino* speaks of ASARCO, that is the entity to which he refers, and the Mr. Lees who turns the unemployed miners out into the snow is a real-life character, all of which raises some interesting questions.

The book is beautiful, so would we rather have the novel or the miners' health and happiness? Obviously we can't have both. Are the actions of our government in any way ours? To what extent have our policies changed?

Carlos Montemayor never poses such questions, and one can yield completely to this novel's esthetic charms, which go so far beyond the ordinary, yet it would be remiss of me as translator not to point out that *Gambusino* belongs to us as much as it does to Mexico. It is one of our historic children.

—John Copeland

For Martha Beatriz.
And in memory of
Bernabé Moyers, who
was the first to speak to me
of gambusinos.

Gambusino. Masculine. Mineralogy. Experienced miner who spends his time searching for mineral deposits. Applies especially to those who go in search of placer gold.

It appears that its origin was one of so many perverse Castilianizations of English in the north. In Baja California they also say *cambusino*, which suggests the presence of the English words *can* (poder) and *buy*, for *to busy* (ocupar), pronounced *bisi* or *busi* as is common among the uneducated. *Cambusino* might have been said by the first seekers of North American gold in the frontier region; individuals who *occupied* themselves as workers or explorers in mining and who afterwards were adventurers who went in search of business of that character, on behalf of the companies of their own nationality which had managed to monopolize said exploitation. Nevertheless, I think it more likely that *gambusino* comes from the English *to gamble* (jugar). And I also believe that this explanation is the one which most nearly approximates the nomadic nature of the term. A *gamblebusiness* must be an individual who plays at negotiations, who stakes all on a deal, or who is inspired by risk; an adventuring negotiator, a worker who participates in adventures, or an adventurer who works.

—*Diccionario de Mejicanismos* by Franciso J. Santamaría

The Past

I

In Villa Ocampo Alfredo Montenegro knew the fury of the mines. For him the odor of carbide was familiar, the roar of cave-ins, the suffocating heat of the shafts and the galleries, the water which rotted the earth, the boots, men's lungs. He'd also learned from his father to compete with the gambusinos, those seekers of deposits hidden as if at the end of dreams, that vanished or crystalized, subject only to the yoke of persistence. In Villa Ocampo he saw the natives who worked in the mines crossing the town as if they were far off and had no knowledge of the mining. Through them he'd learned about death for the first time while still a child when his father's helper Jacinto died. Before he found Jacinto shrouded and stretched out on the floor crosswise to the ceiling beams, below which the natives drank among the flowers and candles, he had seen him alive, lying on the ground on top of blankets. Jacinto had opened his eyes to look at him, and Alfredo had seen the eyes, which were large and red, move across his face without stopping. He'd drawn closer and taken hold of a long, calloused hand and managed to feel a small tremor in it.

"Jacinto," he said. "Jacinto!" he cried.

It was the first time he had known silence, that between his hands, in spite of his young age, the world was anchored in silence.

A year later his mother brought him to Parral, and there they stayed for a full year in his grandparents' house. Often he and I went with Pastor Ramírez to the old house where Methodist services were held. The odor of flowers, readings from the Bible, the flocks of goats from Palestine, slowly covered my life also. Occasionally Alfredo would explain the versicles as signs of his own destiny: *In the plain of Jordan did the king cast them, in the clay ground between Succoth and Zarthan. And Solomon left all the vessels unweighed, because they were exceeding many: neither was the weight of the brass found out.* He knew that Succoth and Zarthan were nothing like Villa Ocampo, or anywhere near here, but he had a premonition that the light and the clean earth which he saw the first time he went with Jacinto to the old mine shafts in Villa Ocampo were the same as those between Succoth and Zarthan. And he visualized smelting in terms of the things his father taught him: the lead burning as it fell in the natural molds of the earth, like the tears of the world.

His grandfather died when we were very small. I only remember a night at the railway station: an enormous silhouette, a reddish face leaning over him. When we were twelve his grandmother died. Alfredo and I were there when Pastor Ramírez gathered with three or four Methodist families on a cold gray February day in the biting wind. The graveyard, the hills, the gray sky looked desolate; the body of his grandmother was lowered into the hard earth, already old, useless now for living and useless for the cold winter wind. She was the last of his mother's relatives who lived here. The relatives of don Esteban, his father, lived in Nuevo León, in towns and cities that Alfredo would never visit, nor from which any friendly word would ever come. His parents arrived three days after the burial. At the end of a few weeks, after selling the grandfather's properties, they returned to Villa Ocampo and Alfredo stayed on, living with Pastor Ramírez.

On certain nights Alfredo felt for the first time that he was a lonely trunk deprived of the community by which the grass is nurtured, or the leaves and branches that together mass in a tree and seize life in their arms; he knew the bittersweet taste of surviving alone in spite of his youth, in spite of the preachings of Pastor Ramírez, amidst the constant strife of being the only Protestant in school and having to fight daily to defend himself against us, making his way a step at a time.

At the beginning of 1929 Alfredo left the studies we had begun together in Chihuahua and returned with his father to dismantle the mine in Villa Ocampo. Without success they explored the various strata of the vein. All that remained of metal in the mine was in the pillars, where the cost of extraction was now prohibitive. His father intended to go to the sierras, to Los Azules, but returned to Parral with his sick mother. Don Esteban worked for San Francisco Mines and Co. and later helped found cooperatives with other owners of mining properties. When Alfredo's mother died, the situation of the mining companies was very precarious. The depreciation of silver that year increased the problems of the union members, the workers' assemblies, and the misery of all the mining towns.

In September Alfredo decided to work in Villa Escobedo, for American Smelting; Superintendent Lees had offered him work in Veta Grande, the principal mine of the area. Within a very short time the company scaled back work in the mine, announcing the layoff of many miners. Alfredo's father said there was nothing more to be done here and that they ought to leave right away. Alfredo believed it would be impossible to get the mine running again, but told me, *This is my first chance to work alone. I don't want to stop again just when I've started.*

One month later American Smelting dismissed more than fifteen hundred miners. The next day, when the superintendent came out of the City Hall, he was surrounded by the workers and it was feared that he might be hurt. Troops from the army arrived to prevent attacks against mining installations or against North American personnel. It was the first of November, the Day of the Dead. Families arrived at the cemetery to tend the graves as if they had come to say goodbye to themselves, to the streets, to their homes. Alfredo discovered that the silence of the land when the mines ceased to work hurt, wounded him profoundly.

At the end of a few days the life of the village changed: the silence, the haste, the closing of businesses, the scarcity of fuel. Starting on the twelfth of November, the laid-off miners began to beg for food in the streets. They received help only from those who still worked in the nearby mines, in the dismantling, or in guarding the installation at Veta Grande. Two days later they woke up to find the mountains white with snow. Alfredo felt forlorn in the snow, was prey to an anguish that filled him because of the beautiful whiteness of the snow over the desolate town, over its snowy streets where men and women were begging food. Along the roads to San Francisco del Oro, to Santa Bárbara, to Parral, Alfredo saw families moving, dragging children and little bundles of clothes down the whitest byways, some stopping at places they had cleared of snow to make a warmer spot to sit down to await the passing of their fatigue, of their hunger.

I remember there were shutdowns and reorganizations in several parts of the state. Some companies charged the miners for medical aid and medicines that were given to them while working for the company, with the result that you saw sizeable groups leaving the sierra without money, wandering lost along the highways until they reached Parral or San Francisco del Oro. In several places children were hired for sixteen hour work days and their salaries reduced to fifty percent of the minimum. Many caravans were jammed together on the snowy highways, in the streets, congregations of defenseless families. These were difficult days. My family was affected too; my father's business declined and I returned to Parral for a year.

It was during that period I visited Alfredo. In the afternoons we would walk with Andrés through the silent buildings of what had been the North American colony, seeing the houses of the town below, their angular roofs. We walked through the mills, past the mine entrances, checking on the security guards. Alfredo knew, through his father, that the mines would not reopen. They had talked about it one of those first afternoons, but Andrés just laughed agreeably, slowly, without believing it. It was already winter. The town looked dim, had a dream-like quality as if it were unaware of its surroundings and of what nurtured it. *You get attached too much and you lose. Everything gets pretty quiet; you're not really choosing. Then your life is something which just happens to you and isn't yours,* his father had told him. And he lived out this prediction a step at a time, feeling his attachment to custom: the noise of the mills, the dusty earth, the residue of the mine blown over everything. Little by little the watchmen found themselves with nothing to do because the miners, their families, and various merchants started moving away from the hunger of Nuevas Minas toward Parral or Santa Bárbara, some even further.

The noise of the mine works being dismantled was different, the sounds of the machinery, the ore, the tracks, the supplies increasing with the clamor of departing families. It was as though the veins and the tendons of Villa Escobedo had broken through to the surface. Machinery and equipment which had been introduced into the mine were once again being damaged by the effort of getting them out, releasing an odor of echoes, the silent murmur of water which inundates and asphyxiates, that rots the earth in the darkness of its veins. The empty houses left along the streets and on the hills themselves appeared to withdraw, the walls to fill themselves with gradual forgetfulness; the railway station was dismantled and from then on a few needy families worked in the abandoned shafts. I returned to Chihuahua to study and left Alfredo once again. My father sold my grandparents' house. It was the beginning of 1931. Alfredo still held on at "Minas Nuevas," as the old people continued to call Villa Escobedo.

He left there in 1933, the same year in which I returned from my studies. I couldn't see him immediately. They gave me the position of teacher in Santa Bárbara so that for half a year I was rooted there. These were the months, I believe, in which Alfredo came to understand his ambitions, his personality, his stubborn egotism. The poverty of the streets and the mines made him feel wounded and impotent, filling him with rancor toward the company and the region generally. With a cold intelligence he understood, without looking further than what worked or caused sadness, fear or disaster, that life was not a force that was able to make sense of itself through a group or a body politic, or that unions could resolve, that misery could elevate to the level of conscience: that it was simply the impulse of a fistful of human bodies, miserable and unlike each other, placed like objects in the impersonal hills where they were disposed to live, to unite in order to survive at whatever price; a fistful of bodies attached by a painful life to the ground, to an irrational heat in order that among those subterranean corridors and in the corrosive desert dirt, life might bloom and continue to bloom, oppressed not so much by ideas or by loss of heart, not so much by ancestors buried at the foot of the mine or by the landscape, ideas or birth; no, but by work, by the search for bread, by the blind struggle to conquer hunger so that the people could continue here in the hills like the humidity under the grass, like the humidity of our feelings under life. He held fast in that solitary struggle, feeling the resentment and poverty of a miner thrown on the most ample plain of time, of rivers, seeking a grain of pure gold, the all-powerful vein in the silence of the earth. It was late to do anything else; it was late at the age of twenty-eight to make a whole new start; he felt the urgency to live, to return a mine to production, he, who from the beginning of his lonely work had seen mines wear out, flood, knowing that he also had to live, to resurrect himself, to trod his earth, his rocks, as if he trod his days, his birth, his death.

In San Francisco del Oro he said goodbye to his father. He remained in Parral, working with Manuel Robles before going to the mines the latter owned near Durango. Don Esteban left for Los Azules. When they said goodbye, Alfredo felt a surge of pride at being a miner like his father, at being complete within himself and stubborn, at being for the first time himself and totally on his own.

"Life is hard now," don Esteban had said. "Yes, I really think it is. It's not enough to want to live, to want to work, son. Life is clearly not always easy. It's not enough just to want something. Who would have thought that now even I find it hard to get ahead. All of us have been hurt, or most of us at least. We never should have left Ocampo. We ought not to have come."

Alfredo returned to Parral and that was the occasion of our meeting again. He, as I said, did not want to work in the mines for others, but on his own. He began, nevertheless, from that time forth to help Robles. I know that Alfredo did not envy my employment, much less the lamentable poems I had begun to write. When I showed them to him, he looked at me amazed, waiting for me to explain why I was doing it, since that was not work.

It was the month of September. Heavy rains fell. The river rose above the bridges one night and flooded the streets, forming whirlpools and toppling the poorer houses, dilapidated walls. We surveyed the town with Pastor Ramírez, helping miners in the neighborhoods of La Peña, El Ojito, and Guanajuato. Parral was taking in the hungry, those who were fired, laid off, flooded out, *but it did not let itself sink,* said Alfredo, *get knocked down or give up the fight.*

Four months later he met Irene, also a Methodist. Her people came from Coahuila, from Monclova, I think. She was fair, tall, with green eyes. In the religious services I went to with Alfredo, she sang very sweetly. For a long time she resisted his courtship and also mine. But that year life was still difficult; the Methodists were few. Irene was the first to mention there were no women in church, saying Alfredo had no alternative to her. He insisted that was not true. But he was incapable of looking for another woman outside the church. At that time he was incapable of departing from what he had been since boyhood. Maybe he didn't exactly seek Irene for religious reasons, but certainly for the character implied by being a Methodist in those days.

At the beginning of October the following year he and Irene left Parral, bound for Durango and the Robles mine. When we said goodbye, Alfredo was already a stubborn man, a seeker after the vein that one feels in the blood like a voice, like a memory equal to the sudden sensation of having lived through a moment, of waiting for the descent of a time one feels he has already lived, like a town or a landscape one crosses yet again.

Now, thirty years later, in the weeks prior to his return to Minas Nuevas, Alfredo felt much less time had passed, that he had been marching more slowly or more fleetingly, until there remained only the warm, useless dust. Now after thirty years, while he spoke of his plans with the boy, he felt that Minas Nuevas was not another beginning, but one long day without rest, a circular track that persisted in him as if both were one and the same, and only now did he understand that it was destiny, a preordained course like the duration of the day or the roads of a given town, because destiny is a lifestyle, a hope that suddenly the body remembers in a way which we don't think is possible, without sounds, without words, without thoughts. *Thirty years,* he told me. *Thirty years,* he also said on the night he crossed the dry river bed, on returning home. He relived the first moment in which he abandoned Minas Nuevas, without knowing by what roads in his body he had arrived back again at such abandonment: an anxiousness to leave, a feeling that jerked the roots of the mine from his soul, from the leaving, *even though I might be alone,* he told me, *even though something might break in me and I'd stop searching. Even though it meant I would wait in a closed house and look out through the window at the streets, at the other houses, at other summers, feeling the same resentment.*

The Present

I

"They're gambusinos," Alfredo answered. "Those are the fires of prospectors. There must be seven, or more."

Alfredo had been watching them; the distant fires were weak lights sliding through the hills toward the north of the valley where the ruins of Villa Escobedo were. Alfredo looked at his own fire, which was burning peacefully as all campfires do, the only odor coming from the coffee that was heating.

"It's the best I can expect, kid . . ." he continued. "But I feel sorry for those I know. Not for myself, but for others." Alfredo closed his eyes. Lying down next to the odor of the fire, he saw neither the earth nor the sky, but was aware of the innumerable sounds of the night, of the stars, as if the earth knew of the fatigue in the lives of those it contained. "Don't try to understand what I said, kid. You need to be older, that's all."

The boy poured more coffee into his cup. The bundles of tools left a faint profile on the ground near the mules. He remembered his village, the dirt road down which he moved toward Talamantes de Arriba, feeling the night clotted around him, the silence in the middle of the road, and Amelia, her long hair, her bare feet walking along the river bank. Several times he saw her at nightfall when the warm earth of Talamantes was alive with the uninterrupted sounds of heat, of pleasure, of young men moving by feel through the darkness, like the covers of many dark pieces of furniture which hide in the earth, along with their desires. *Who would have thought it; who was going to say that I would be here?* he thought. *One day my brothers will come . . . I did it alone,* he repeated for his own benefit. He turned to Alfredo and spoke to him without receiving a reply. He told him that he needed to succeed, that it didn't matter how long it took, that he needed to come out well, and in some obscure way he was put in touch with his village, with Ana. He'd left Talamantes without really wanting to abandon the sweet earth of Ojo de Agua, the misery with which all covered themselves, as with warm blankets.

"It's better that you stay here," his father said several years ago, the last night on which they spoke. "If you want work, don't think you can't find it here. With the Ruizes you could make two or three trips a day, Jesús. Because you learn to live wherever you are. Anyone who is born already knows how to live. It's a question of standing up to things, and that you've already learned here."

The ranch was enough for his father and brothers. But between Ojo de Agua and Talamantes there was no chance to work or to live. *I will not only work with Refugio,* the boy thought that night. *I can also work in the mine or at Triplay, or learn something else. Somewhere else things are going on, not here.*

His father lifted the cup of coffee; he finished drinking, but continued with the cup suspended and did not speak again. It was as if his father had already decided how to manage without him, as if he had already divided the work of sowing the crops between his two younger sons.

"Yes, I have lived here all my life," his father continued. "I can't be moving around just for the sake of it. There in Parral the river only has water when it rains. But the one we have here runs all the time. I'm like that. Like a spring of water, I keep going where I am, without having to change villages. How can this land harm me? Parral doesn't know you; you don't belong. Here when you sow in the earth, it's like an agreement. It's as if you said to it, 'Give me a fistful of this and one of that, and I will give you in exchange this and this other.' But Parral has been reduced to bones. It's no good for anything; you can only feel sorry for it."

It was October, the boy thought. *Yes, it was October.* On the old wooden table, which was covered with a stained linen tablecloth, were some quinces his brother Julián had brought that afternoon. A few feet from the door was the road, the dust, the dog stretched out on the ground where the reflection of the oil lamp barely reached him. The boy was smoking, hearing the noise of the crickets and feeling the fresh breeze, warm still, but also already fresh, that entered through the open door. *It was October,* he thought. A few weeks earlier in the González orchard the walnut trees had been full of nuts; during several days they had beat them down; it was the last work he did with his brothers. He thought of the fallen branches, of the dry leaves that had separated from the trees, the apple trees, the peach trees, and the sudden freezing wind that had begun to blow at five in the morning from the bend in the river to the north, from where you could hear the bellowing of the cattle going by the houses in Talamantes. That morning he had gone with his brother Julián to the central plaza. At the bakery ovens he had seen Amelia; her loose hair covered her shoulders. But that night a very light wind blew along the road. Julián had nodded off at the table and remained so, leaning on his arms. His hat was pushed back, his face tired, dusty, and a slight snore escaped from his open mouth as he breathed. His father had spat on the earthen floor. He also looked outside, toward the night, holding his empty cup.

"Money does me no good now, Jesús," said his father, speaking again. "It was good when there was still a whole town. Now no, son. And you don't know anything about money. That's why you don't understand why you're going . . . But take care of yourself because your life is part of the little that's left. You're one of the few who were born here."

But it was not fear, thought the boy; *it was not fear.* It was abandoning his little town, yes, and in that his father was right; it was feeling the money of Parral was something unknown, of crossing its streets with a hat pushed back on his head, with worn boots and his hands stuck in his pockets as if there he carried his life and was protecting it; it was feeling that he proved himself by stopping on bridges and in the streets, by entering cheap places to eat a fistful of meat with a certain enjoyment at conquering, of having withstood the danger of exposing himself to the people, as if it gave him a secret triumph and his life were now more extensive, more enviable. *But it was not fear,* he repeated, looking at the fires of the gambusinos in the distance. *No, no, it was not fear,* he said again as he lay down, seeing Alfredo silhouetted against the earth, the body of Alfredo stiller and smaller, already not even a bundle of rocks or of dirt, but a little piece of wall which had fallen years ago, like the foundations of the ruins of Talamantes or Villa Escobedo. *It's that we realize so little. Now I understand why I had to leave, now, in spite of Alfredo and Ana. Yes, I did it. I succeeded, without fear. In spite of Alfredo, although it might be hard for him to admit it.*

"No, it's not fear, Alfredo," he said aloud. "I assure you it isn't."

When he spoke, he heard again the abiding sounds of the earth, of insects which were like a fist that knocked clearly at his chest, monotonous as the sound of the stars, like the coals of his fire that had begun to go out. Lying down, closing his eyes, he felt sleep on his forehead, not like the odor of Ana that arrived smoothly at his face before her body embraced him, but like a violent hand, complete sleep, sudden; and much later he heard again the noise of the earth, the sound of the stars, smelled the odor of burnt wood where many coals beat like memories in someone who sleeps: and he was not able to understand that it was an anguish which was blossoming in him for the first time, like the bitterness of the quince that night when he had talked with his father years ago; he didn't know how many now, seven, eight perhaps. And that memory began to fall from the stars so that all the time that it took to reach him, to the very bottom of his soul, would be the length of his life; that he might realize the earth is sometimes sweet, other times bitter, and still others the abyss where man, although he lies motionless in his grave, only is what falls, what falls again loosened from an old dry tree, like one piece more of the earth, until he vanishes in the heart of the wind, in the heart of a dream in which all men are fleetingly equal in order that they might learn to fall, to hear their fall, to form part of the silence like water which evaporates, like the rocks or the dust.

The Past
II

That day in San Francisco del Oro, he told me that he had walked down with his father from the St. Luis Company to the main street. The morning was very clear, but Alfredo felt it was gray and sordid because of the narrow dirty streets and the oppression he sensed in the men in their miserable homes in the ravines.

"To tell the truth, it bothers me that you still won't give up your hopes about Veta Grande," his father had said. "The Ocampo business is finished. I have no further hopes, at least in that quarter. Either we go to Los Azules or we'll have to search for some other site in Ojinaga or towards Durango. But the same thing will happen here, and in Santa Bárbara. It doesn't look good to me that they brought troops to Minas Nuevas; soldiers among hungry miners without work is not a good thing. It's not necessary, like the coup de grâce, like insisting someone should fall down when he has already been on the ground a long time."

A freezing wind insisted on swelling itself with the dust in the street and in stabbing at faces, bodies, poor walls. The heat of the kitchen where they went to eat was quite unexpected. They sat down at the back near the fire.

"We came here originally for your mother," don Esteban continued. "Now there's no reason to stay anyplace. After all, what is a place? Work pops up everywhere. We can't stay where a vein has run out, where everyone is starving. Somewhere else a vein is bound to be discovered and life will begin again, work. We can't go on this way because it's like being beaten and hidden away, like sitting in the shade, waiting for nothing. Why are these miners leaving Villa Escobedo? If they remained here, they would die. They're also going to endure hardship somewhere else, but now this is happening even to me. I'm here now, sticking it out where everything has already dried up. No, no, son, we both ought to understand. If you stay with a woman or with work that are no longer yours, then it's just a way of hiding yourself from what you might do, or already know, and you're finished; yes, you've already dropped your hands and are not aware of anything. I feel obligations to my friends, to the projects with the bank and the cooperative. I know that if we had been lucky, there would have been a lot of money. But I am not in favor of these things. I could do it, but I'm not in favor of it. I only want to do what I have to do. Because I'm tired of what doesn't concern me directly. Others are willing to be subject to circumstances that involve their feelings because it hurts them to leave the place where they are hidden because there is a warmth in the customs which seem more important than their individual lives. Such attachment is accepting defeat and not a thing of the will; it is something that happens to you, not that you cause. And during the little time that we're here on earth, son, we ought to live well, or try to live well, try to do things, not allow them simply to fall on us so all we do is pick up the pieces, meek laborers, workers in a hungry and badly paid life."

One week earlier don Esteban had been in Jiménez with the group commissioned to deliver the proposals of the cooperative to Governor León. But the misery was palpable in the streets, in the cities. Alfredo felt confusedly that his life had begun on these same terms, that he was beginning to feel his way to a place where things didn't simply happen, but where he guided or unchained them. Obscurely he felt the need to separate himself from his father, to open a path that wouldn't hold them together as they had been up to now, that wouldn't make them one, father and son, but related men already isolated. When they went out to eat, they said goodbye in the middle of the street; Alfredo kissed him on the cheek and his father rested his hand on Alfredo's shoulder. Only years later, about 1940, would they meet again in Durango.

"Poverty doesn't matter to me," don Esteban had said. "Everything has been bad since Veta Grande, son. But I did the best I could wherever I was. It's good to know how to die the way a man should, being where he should be, knowing one has done his best."

And his pride that Alfredo was his son was like an anchor, the knowledge his stubborn blood would live on, confronting the things of life as the days do our bodies, wearing them out, breaking them, leaving them in pieces. He felt that it was the miners, not life's peons, not life's badly paid workers, but men like Alfredo who were chosen to wound the subterranean darkness where all men will be deposited, the darkness which is opened by the luminous violence of having participated in the battle against life, against the grasping hands which always retain life, but cannot hold us.

And that was Alfredo. That was his position, his conscience. Not to be subject to any other thing or place, but to remain his own man for that combat, for that search that was deeper than loneliness, more benign than understanding or memory. That's me, he told me many times, as if it were an itinerary or a recognition—drunk, calm, content—*this is what I am, Armando, the only way I can make sense of things: looking for veins, touching rocks, clearing things out of my way, struggling.* He understood that his life in Ocampo, his boyhood among the mines where his father worked when he learned to feel the intensity of the search and of work, the misery of the miners of Veta Grande, the death of the streets and the men of Villa Escobedo—were his first sips of the liquor of life, the bitter liquor of the will, of the dark force by which men are able to define themselves.

The Present
II

Alfredo shouted from the door of the shop. Once more he said to get away from the boy, to stop bothering him.

"He doesn't know anything about mines. Ask me, old man," he shouted again.

The boy heard him from the ruined plaza, seated on a bench in the midst of the warm sounds of the earth. Several children were playing next to the remains of a statue of General Escobedo.

"It's silver, it's a vein of silver. I've already told you," Alfredo added.

"I was talking to him about the mines around here," answered the old man, who raised his hand to his hat, tipping it so that he could include a view of the shop.

Old Andrés went over to the boy and sat down on the same bench. Alfredo remained in the door of the shop. Someone asked him for cigarettes and he took a package out of his shirt. The boy crossed the street. Alfredo looked at him with reddened eyes, with a face that was euphoric, arrogant, his whole being suffused with the richness of the vein, with a desire to boast. The sun fell like lead on the boy. Alfredo, outside the door, remained in a fringe of shade. The boy turned again toward the plaza. Old Andrés was waiting for him on the bench.

"I don't want to spend any more time here," said the boy, in a low voice while he took out two cigarettes. "I'm tired, Alfredo."

"I don't want to spend time here either, kid. Believe me, I've had enough." Then he took a step forward, directing himself toward Andrés. "Old fellow! Do you want another beer?"

The old man refused with a wave of his hand. Alfredo stood for an instant longer in the doorway, looking at the plaza.

"The road will be hard going at this time of day," said the owner of the shop when Alfredo resumed his position against the counter. The proprietor took the least warm beer from the shelf and placed it in front of him. Alfredo took a long swallow from the bottle. "Now all the mines around here are flooded," the owner continued. "There would be many problems in working them again, don't you think? Andrés says there's a lot more minerals than just those abandoned pillars."

"Andrés is stubborn," Alfredo answered. "He never has wanted to understand." He left the empty bottle on the counter, next to a glass of dried herbs. "How much do I owe you?"

"Ten pesos. No, twelve."

He left the shop. He felt a wave of heat as he stepped down into the dust of the street. The boy was sitting on the same bench, smoking with the old man. The mules were quiet, as if tuned to the noises of the earth. The ruins of City Hall, the boarded-up windows, the muted sounds of the distant voices of children, the summer—all passed through Alfredo as if he had opened his eyes after many years in the same place, opened his days like rocks without walls, without nuclei.

"Stubborn old man, that's what you are. You're a stubborn old man, Andrés," said Alfredo, when he was near them. "You're the same as you were thirty years ago, only older."

"As a young man, everyone looked stupid to you," the old man answered. "Now they look older."

Alfredo crossed the square. They went down the street toward the statue of General Escobedo. The animals drank from a fountain overflowing with water. Alfredo and the boy washed their arms and faces. For Andrés the vein could only be in one of two places, if it weren't a branch of Veta Grande. *But it is a branch,* he thought, *it has to be an offshoot of Veta Grande.*

"It can only be in two places," he told them, while Alfredo and the boy dried their faces with their shirt sleeves, "in Tambor Hill or in Potro Hill. And those are near Veta Grande."

"You'll see, old man," answered Alfredo. "Get used to the idea this town will live better. We'll feed everyone with this vein. They'll eat out of our hands. That's what should matter to them."

They got on their mules. Alfredo looked at the frail, aged body of Andrés. Then he turned toward the end of the street. To his left he saw the eroded hills of the mines, the streets of the abandoned town. They crossed the dry bed of the arroyo and went up through the ruins of the railway station. They saw the cemetery with its rough thickets and broken rocks. They detoured to avoid a ravine and passed some distance from the ruins of the church. It was too late for the trip to Parral. The summer seemed to fall like burning bricks on their shoulders, on their legs. The cicadas droned in the grass. Alfredo caressed the neck of the mule. The warm hide of his mount was shining. The road appeared to drop as it narrowed, and Alfredo went ahead with the mule that carried the rock samples.

There were many mines, all small and poor, which had been worked out in their turn. There were many places where he had felt powerless and deeply resentful. It pained him to have to struggle again through the land where they found the vein. Now, under a crushing sun on a burning day, he wanted to look through the window of life at all his years, at those of all of us his friends, his children, at all that didn't matter but which he did of necessity in order to survive. At this point nothing mattered. He glanced at the sun, high in a cloudless sky, a sun that flamed, eroded heaven itself, burning his hair. He closed his eyes, which were involuntarily filled with warm tears. He tried to open them again and look at the sun, to look fixedly at it, to feel that it was the source of the heat which fell over all things, not only on themselves, not just on the road. He felt exhilarated by the sun on his face, by his eyes blinded by tears. *I've been doing the same thing a long time,* he told me that same day. *It's a long time to want something, Armando, to wait for something.*

At about two in the afternoon they arrived at a crossing of canals that were near the roads of the neighborhood. They slid down off their tired animals as if an avalanche of thoughts or of life were about to fall. The mules were very sweaty. After these had drunk in the canal, the men threw themselves in the water. Alfredo felt that the coolness of the water in his hair, on his neck, soaking his shirt, was falling in some interior part of himself, as if within himself a deep peace took hold. Then they sat down on the ground in the shade of the scanty trees with a small bottle of mezcal, as if they had come from very far away and thirst had risen in their bodies from the calm; and they heard the earth, the grass, the rocks. Meanwhile, in the gathering confusion of their fatigue, they spoke without object of the months of work locating the vein, the passing of days, of hunger, of the summer.

"We'll do it, yes," Alfredo said again. "It's late, but we will do it. What I said to you this morning didn't make sense, kid. Those were doubts, nothing more, but I was mistaken. I was exaggerating things," he insisted again. "All we need is a deal, any deal. This has happened on other occasions. I know it has. There won't be a problem. In these cases the concession the government grants for mining has nothing to do with the land where the vein is found. We wouldn't be able to exploit it, but then neither would the Chávezes. A working arrangement is what we need, yes, a working arrangement."

The boy thought their conversation of the morning was no different, that he was saying the same thing as now; it hadn't changed.

"I'll look for don Enrique right away," Alfredo added. "Everything will be all right. You'll see. Everything will be settled."

The boy continued to pay attention until finally he was staring fixedly, without hearing, conscious of the sound of the water in the canal, of the aroma of the earth, of the trees where they rested. An hour later he opened his eyes, aware of the noise of the heat rising from the earth. He awoke with the deafening weight of summer on his forehead, like the hardest hand that tries to break your bones and to take your disordered dream with its fingers and plunge it deeper into the body, into the dusty, sweaty clothing. He saw Alfredo lying there with his mouth half open and his salt and pepper beard full of dust. He got up and shouted at him and continued shouting until he saw the other move. Alfredo opened his eyes, making an effort to get up and to wake himself up completely, brushing the dirt from his face. The animals were watching with their large dark eyes blinking, chewing their bits. It was late and having drunk mezcal they felt even hungrier. Alfredo took the reins of the mule which carried the rock samples. They left the canals, walking toward the road. Alfredo felt the sweat on his hands, on the damp reins with which he controlled the mule as though it were his life, as if this way he controlled his days. He looked at the saddlebags again, the glistening hairy body of the animal, the docility with which it moved.

They arrived at the highway along which the buses that ran to San Francisco del Oro and to Santa Bárbara stopped to pick up passengers from the outlying ranches. There they had coffee and meat. They heard the noise of motors again, of townspeople, of the asphalt highway. The boy spoke and Alfredo also became animated, as if for a moment they had truly rested, as if something had joined them in a sudden pardon. Before resuming their trip, they saw people getting in and out of buses. They saw more people arriving on foot from every direction and waiting together for the next wave of transports, and then boarding them in turn: the heat, the goodwill of people when they don't know what they are giving, when they don't know they are being generous.

open, their lips thick and unmoving. Now in the tunnel they moved without strength, wishing perhaps to sleep in the midst of all the other miners, to feel their companions around them, to hear everyone, to feel themselves embraced, to touch living flesh. They crossed the gallery; they looked at the shining, jumbled, still metal, as if the mine had felt the cave-in and knew of the catastrophe; they moved slowly, sustained by the warmth and the smell of the other miners; they came up to their companions who had fainted and moved on toward the light; they left the shaft, trod the ground outside, where there was a different silence in the air, air everywhere. They arrived at the bunkhouses and went in by themselves. The murmur from miners in the camp increased little by little. The afternoon had passed. The miners from the third shift gradually arrived. All those from the morning shift were outside, eating or drinking coffee, smoking, sitting on the ground near the sheds, to one side of the ore trucks. Night had fallen. There was a full moon.

His son slept in the bunkhouse that he and his partners occupied. Part of the night Alfredo and his associates were in the camp, checking the zone of the cave-in with a crew of drillers. They worked several hours. Around midnight Alfredo returned to the bunkhouse. His son was still sleeping. He sat down on his cot to rest, closing his eyes, waiting for his son to wake up so he could take him home. He felt the fatigue. He thought about many things, heard a clamor inside himself from many places, as if it were an incoherent baggage he carried year after year, during sleep, during work. After a long time he opened his eyes. He was aware of a heavy silence around himself and his arms felt hard, tense. Once more he heard the noise from the generating plant, the hubbub of the camp on the night air. He felt an oppression in his chest; on closing his eyes, he believed he was falling down a well, and a dizziness made him sweat. A warm fist, a hand seized him roughly by the hair, by the neck, a burning fist that made him sleep, stunned by the thoughts and the voices that poured over him, in his abyss. When he tried to open his eyes and fix them on the door of the bunkhouse, a multitude of places and roads interposed themselves, and at the bottom there was a deep calm; he felt the circulation of his blood in his body and felt his thoughts run free, as if nothing had happened, nothing more than an awareness of the weight of his soul, of his sleep, of his feelings. He looked at the rough wood, the thick boards; then he lowered his gaze and looked at his legs, his body, his hands on the bed, unfeeling, full of sleep, of strange dominions; he looked at the muddy miner's boots on his feet, which were placed on the floor. The lamp remained lit. He got up. Two hours had passed.

He woke up his son, and they went out of the bunkhouse to get in one of the trucks. On crossing the camp, Alfredo enjoyed the freshness of the night. The miners' bunkhouse was dark. There was light in the entrance to the shafts and in the watchmen's shacks. The sheds with the ore trucks appeared pale in the light of the moon, which seemed to be bursting in the center of the sky. He liked to walk this way through the camp at night, listening to the noise of the crickets, of the air, of the mine. He felt the nights were limitless and wanted to be awake in them, to experience everything.

The boy did not go back to sleep. He looked through the open window of the truck at the hills, at the lights of the surrounding villages, at the moonlight falling on the earth, on the night in these places, as if a candle were lit behind the curtain of space and shone through. While he drove, his son's gaze was fixed on him for some time; Alfredo felt the boy's unquestioning eyes, the purity of his glance, a profundity that disarmed him.

From his partners and from himself, Alfredo's son had learned the workings of the mine: the vein, the drilling, the strata. I remember the rapidity with which he learned these things, and the way they interested him. He accompanied Alfredo in the ore trucks, with the gangs and to all the different levels. He swung a pick near the lamps with the miners. But it was more important that he understand the vein, pinpointing the metals and the strata: the work of a mining man. He witnessed paydays with the same surprise I did; he looked at the lines of miners with their powerful voices, the laughter, the jests, the protests. Alfredo wanted his son to understand the mine as a whole, with its unskilled laborers, its installations, the shipments to the mills, and above all the vein, the trajectory and the exploration of the buried vein beyond the mine, in the memory of the body or of the blood.

Near the tenth year the vein ran out. The disorder in the earth, the silence, found a mirror in the dry, yellow grass. They shut down the camp in four months. His son helped daily while the tracks were dismantled, the crossties taken up. The network of lights became a mess of trodden crystal, white, a soul impregnating the rocks with each roll of wire which was taken from the wall, amidst the metal, in the galleries, stained, made one with the corrosive water. The gangs did the bulk of the work. Alfredo and his partners made an inventory of all stock on hand, tools, and equipment. They remained in the camp night and day until everything was finished. The transports left with full loads, with the dissected camp wrapped in sacking, mixed among the iron, the wire, and the wood. On the ground there remained forgotten signs of the bunkhouses and trash.

At night coffee was made and meat spread on a hot stove. Afterwards they would sit around the stove and smoke, talking of the mine, of the installations, of the problems among the miners; or speak of Parral, remembering places, people, as if Parral had eyes, a face that looked at the flat, thirsty sky, which seemed to collapse on the hills and knew what the men did wherever they went. When his fellow workers slept, Alfredo made the rounds of the camp, the entrances to the shafts. The hills, profiled in the night, seemed to watch him and to sense his thoughts. As he walked, he heard the whisper of stones under his boots, as if they were the scattered minerals of his days, or the echo of his days. He felt his shell slipping away, which for many years time had wounded, a loosening of the roots which grip the soul as tightly as an oak's or the limbs of a woman. It was like the nights in which we used to walk with the watchman at Minas Nuevas and the village seemed to bleed, to wither away slowly below us, like a fistful of glowing insects fallen to the ground in their final moments of life, of memory.

Because in his memory, within himself a man is delicate;

he's used to sticking to his accustomed ways, which are like a drug that habituates him to certain places and a daily routine whose destruction is like ripping out parts of himself which resist withering in the out-of-doors, like the grass and the ground which the wind moves incessantly, as if the wind were a forgetfulness. When day came, when morning spread on the earth of the camp, the mines appeared to forget for a moment that they were dead; for a while they seemed to wait for the noises of a mine, of metal, or blasts, of gangs, until one could only distinguish the vain and insistent sound of the air in space, among the hills.

The last day Alfredo felt the oppression of the camp; the entrances to the shafts appeared to sleep, to withdraw as though they left the colored earth without feeling, without a sign of human life. It was past midday. His son got up in the truck while he decided the order in which the vehicles would leave. The last of the miners crossed from the rear of the camp, walking on the loose stones. Alfredo got into the truck. As they maneuvered to leave in single file, he looked at the earth abandoned to its weight of silence, like any other ground and yet nevertheless distinct, still intense and near; and it is as though the memory can't say goodbye because God, or the universe, has put memory in man for that reason, in order that goodbyes are impossible; one cannot part because things last, not for having bloomed or disappeared, but because they have been part of life, because we have felt them next to our lives, as thousands of flowers each have a life next to all the others, because neither place nor memory are before or after, because they are what matters, because they are sustained by life.

The Present
III

They arrived in Parral in the afternoon. They came in through the loose dust of the first street in the midst of a herd of goats and the shouting boys who cared for them. Alfredo saw the boys were dragging slender switches, their eyes fixed on the goats, which were jostling each other in front of the goatherds. When the goats passed, he pulled on the reins of the mule which carried the rock samples, and they crossed the wide, unpaved street. On hearing the noises of people again, Alfredo felt his breath quicken.

The boy looked toward the railroad tracks. He saw the scattered huts on the hill, far away, one of which would be Ana's. But the euphoria of having returned, of being here once again, of having found not only a vein but more of a life, one that was more complete, began to invade him; and in his heart he felt a seething sense of himself coupled with haste to realize all of it: Talamantes and his memories, the physical desire for Ana, the physical desire to laugh and to get drunk.

They dismounted and left their animals near the bar entrance. The place was crowded. Alfredo took off his hat and passed his hand through hair that was rough, full of dirt from the trip, hardened by sweat. On the earthen floor there was spit, dust, smoked cigarettes. He could hear the ballad "Four Brothers from Guanaceví" from the juke box. The boy continued euphoric, feeling pleasure now in the people and in the music. They ordered beer.

For the first time after so many months of the tepid stuff, cold, bitter, foamy beer ran through their bodies like a sweet perfumed bath reminiscent of adolescence.

"Pepe!" Alfredo cried. "Pepe, service! Two more cups. We need good service!"

Standing up to the bar, they drank two glasses of Las Escobas sotol; then they ordered more beer. The boy enjoyed the people, the noise. Several times he walked to the door, wishing to see the street and the people. He also wanted to make sure of his return, that the mules were still at their posts, that the afternoon and he shared the same life. In the dusty street the mules were securely tied, quiet. But he felt a great peace looking out at the noisy street, as if a silence of distance covered it, while the noise of the canteen dominated and took charge of him, along with the desire to look for Ana, to embrace her, to possess her throughout the hours of the night with all the force of his life. He left the door and put money in the juke box, selecting the same song. Then he went back to Alfredo, who had not sat down. They kicked their boots against the metal bar that was near the floor, several times, as if ridding themselves of the sensation of the road, of having ridden animals. They began to smoke and the shut-in odor of the canteen, of men, of urinals, and of summer increased in strength.

The barkeeper refilled their cups with sotol; he wore a sweaty undershirt and carried a wet rag in one hand; he made conversation with Alfredo, listening to his boasts about the vein, his boundless happiness. The boy, his face sweaty, looked at himself in the mirror located over the shelf of bottles; he saw himself drifting there as in a dream, in another place where he found himself finishing his cup with its flavor of lightly burned water, or water faintly inflamed like a human breath. The ballad "Four Horsemen from Guanaceví" began to play again. The boy remembered the parties with his brothers and his father in Talamantes, the fairs of Valle de Allende.

"Like in Talamantes," said the boy, without addressing himself to anyone in particular, "like in Talamantes when we went to the cockfights and afterwards I went in search of Amelia. More beautiful than Ana. Yes, more beautiful. I'll go looking for her later, by the living God I'll look for her, Alfredo. I want to be with her," he insisted. "I want her to be with me."

Alfredo looked again at the tables, the walls of the canteen, the people. He felt the humiliation which all the days of his life had piled on him, changing his mode of thought, his body, dragging him across the stubborn ground of his years, across time, memories, *until this is where I land,* he told me hours later, *having suffered the rugged country where veins are found, having put up with one more thing . . . Andrés thought I was not going to succeed, but I did. But not only Andrés, everybody: Manuel Robles, Benjamín, Cutberto, Irene . . . All thought I was incapable of doing it.* But he had done it. Yes, so it was. He had done it. I knew that each mine gave him something different, not only a load of metal, but a thought, something internal that was always slightly different.

"It was my money we put into this too," the boy told him slowly, then with an increasing need to reproach, to confront. "We ate all these months, using my money, not only yours, Alfredo. You wouldn't have been able to do this work alone. I'm worth as much as you are now. I am as important as you are. I have worked and endured the same as you. I won't be less in the mine, do you understand? I won't accept it."

"You've earned it, it's true," answered Alfredo. "For a farmer it's too much . . . yes, it's too much."

They drank what remained in their glasses. When Alfredo paid, they crossed the room arm in arm, between the tables. They were in Parral. That's what mattered now. They had returned. But they arrived with a mine in their pockets, under their skins, in their minds, in their breasts, in their mouths. They arrived with the taste of silver, talking and arguing in terms of it. Nothing bothered them but the time which passed without their enjoying it, but the silence which went by without their remembering, knowing it in each part of their bodies. Greed was not a factor, it was an inoffensive animal; for Alfredo it was the pleasure of being a miner once again, of demonstrating feverishly that he still was that. For the boy it was the first moment of feeling himself powerful, astonished by something he didn't understand, that he never had hoped for. It was, principally, his first encounter, his first work, his first inkling that at twenty-nine years of age life had made him a man, had endowed him with an abundance of sudden force, with a firmness he didn't recognize even now, in the moment when he possessed it.

They left at six in the evening. They heard the train

entering the town. The noise grew, stunning the late afternoon, filling it with metal, with whistling, with tracks and earth that trembled as it passed. As it drew near them, the mules retreated against the walls of the houses, and the noise of the cars, of the metal, resembled a rockslide, a continuous explosion in the galleries of a mine that made the dogs howl and bark and the children run toward it from everywhere, as if the world were being invaded by unknown animals that disintegrated deafeningly with the passage of cars stained with oil. The boy remembered that Ana always saw the train go by, loving this commotion, and suddenly he felt an affection for Alfredo, as if he had made the town and the streets shake and everything grow closer and more intimate. As the last car passed, the noise diminished, smothering itself little by little, and the murmur of the town, of the street, returned.

They crossed the railway bridge and continued through the abandoned fields of Botello's orchard. It was the hour at which the workers from La Esmeralda Mine, from San Francisco de Oro, from Santa Bárbara, from Triplay, were coming home. In the midst of the hubbub caused by the people, in the noise of all the pickups, all the buses and bicycles which entered Parral, they crossed the long street, enjoying the early evening together. The animals behaved differently among the automobiles. They went down into the river, heading toward the section of town called Las Quintas, over the loose earth. Beside the dry river bed they saw the orchards, the quiet trees, the branches of the cottonwoods and walnuts moving slightly.

"Wait, kid, let's stop a moment. Here, stop the animals . . ." said Alfredo. "How strange to be here again. I always came back fucked. Not now. Now what happens won't matter, or anything in the future."

While they remained motionless, Alfredo looked at the dry riverbed, at the bridge, at the people, at the children running in the channel. Then he raised his eyes toward the sky. In those moments the sky began to turn more luminous, perfumed, and with the clouds and the faint reddening of the late afternoon the air appeared to take on a new freshness, as if everything were headed toward a sudden quietude or state of blessedness. Flocks of wild doves and crows flew along the river toward the orchards, leaving the walls as if someone had thrown handfuls of stones. Alfredo and the boy felt the clarity of the early evening, with its warm air full of the laughter of children who played in the dirt of the river bed near them, running euphorically as if at every moment their laughter could only increase. As they crossed the channel, there still came from the orchards, the bridge, from Botello's orchard, the confused noise of the town, of the birds, of the automobiles.

They arrived at Alfredo's house and dismounted to open the gate of the corral. On touching the wood, Alfredo felt he was touching a part of himself that was unforgiving and dirty, where the air was unbreathable. That he became witness to a theater of sentiments where remorse took the lead as he entered that patio, that home where he encountered inside himself, in some other part, a place that was closed and monotonous.

"Call your brother so he can help us," he said to his daughter. "Go on, Julia, call him."

He removed the saddlebags from the animals and laid

the rusty tools outside the shed. When he heard the voice of his son and saw him try to lift a weight that was too much for a boy, he himself became the same dull, dirty materials, and he felt that his memories, his dissatisfactions, were like the objects being touched and that because of them he was diminished there in that patio, in that shade, forming with that atmosphere an unworthy brotherhood for being accepting of it.

"It's for you," he told his son later. "Keep this rock in your room. It's silver."

While Jesús busied himself with the animals, he and his son dragged the saddlebags and sacks away. On entering the house, he felt the presence of his wife and a sensation which belonged to the past came back to him, the same distance, the same loosening of everything within himself. It felt as though he were two different men, one who lived mechanically in the moment and the other who awoke and taught him to look, but not to feel the urgency of any thought, of any mine, of any summer or any failure. He noted the slight changes within the house, the places impregnated with familiar odors—all that belonged to him and could no longer be his. He remembered also, behind the mechanism of dimly perceived acts, feelings, and his other homecomings, the encounter with his wife after the death of his first boy in a winter that seemed to freeze each instant, so that they might be kept forever in parts that admitted of no sensation, but could never be forgotten.

The Past
IV

When they left Durango, his first child was just over ten. They arrived in Parral together with Irene's parents, and our friendship took up again where it left off. We enjoyed talking and were together much of the time. Irene was still beautiful. Alfredo worked at buying ore from gambusinos and taking loads of metal from the surrounding mines to the ASARCO mills. But he was tired, as if a stone lay on his chest and caused his glance to follow the wind, the months, as men will do who sit by the side of the road. He felt that after the mines of Ocampo and Durango everything was foreseen; each new mine was only a confirmation of what had preceded it, that stopped time so everything could happen again. By the end of two years he understood more fully the futility of trying to control personal thoughts, anything that went deeper in the brain than the surface. *Nothing has to make sense, nothing,* his father had told him. *Just because a road makes sense if it takes you somewhere, nothing has the obligation to make sense just so you can live in peace. No two things in life are the same.*

Two years later they left Parral and headed for the sierra. He worked with various partners, exploring deposits, getting part of his financing—although he was unaware that

I knew it—from Robles. His family remained in Estación Creel. During the spring and summer of the first year they worked two small copper deposits a few kilometers from the village of Sánchez. When summer was over, he shifted to the Isoguichi region and worked there with no luck through the final months of the year. In autumn, under intense weight of cold, he saw the earth transform itself and the Tarahumara Indians take refuge in canyons and ravines to pass the winter, occupying the caves of animals. Many years earlier, when we were students, we had visited that region. At that time we knew the cold, the silence of the sierra, the loneliness. With winter, the partners left for Parral, to return the following spring, and Alfredo and his son took the train for Estación Creel to rejoin the family.

Almost every morning that winter he went to the Torres general store to drink sotol and talk about the lumberjacks and the miners who worked in the neighborhood. Some Tarahumara Indians who didn't live in the Jesuit centers or were not used by the lumberjacks in their operations, would arrive at the store with some animal skins or other objects they exchanged for food. Then they would disappear into the sierra, into the ravines. The store was always awash with the odors of leather, corn, food cooking, grease, tools; and the flavor of mezcal and conversation made everything seem friendly to Alfredo, from the mere fact that he was part of it. When he walked outside in the late afternoon, the frozen wind struck his face, his flesh, his bones. He would move through the mist as if opening a path to another world, to the years in which we walked together as young men through that same snow, as if the mist were the soul of the outdoors. Going into his house or into the general store, he would be seeking an odor, the mezcal or the boiling coffee that he drank in rapid gulps, feeling the heat in his body, his chest, his stomach, and he would break into a sweat, a different kind of mist in the clarity of the light, in the midst of the heat and smoke from cigarettes and woodstoves, a mist of foreboding or of pleasure.

Come spring, the partners arrived at Estación Creel. Again they went deep into the sierra. Alfredo's son was with them. They went beyond Isoguichi that year, following the horse trails that link Pasigochi, Carichi, Nararachi, Panalachi, and Sánchez. They found few deposits. The last swing they planned was toward Usárare, leaving from Sánchez the third year of the work. They gave up and the partners went their separate ways at the same time the flood occurred in Parral. Irene and the two girls returned to her parents' house, and I went to pick them up at the railway station when they arrived. Within a short time Irene's mother died, and from that time on she remained there with the girls. That year, at the beginning of winter, Alfredo sent word to Irene that their son was ill.

In that season of the year the woods and the ravines appear to be made of copper, the air has a different purity, the Tarahumara Indians fill the village, and the movement of people within the Torres general store shows haste and fatigue. Alfredo's son was sixteen years old. When they went down to Chihuahua to hospitalize him, the streets, the coffee shops, the avenues, the city itself had an air of intimacy which invaded Alfredo's thoughts, carrying him along the paths we followed as students. It would be late when he ceased tramping the dirty, frozen snow, his mind filled with a tenuous dream, with a fullness of something that brought order to those disordered moments—the thing that drove him, that swung him from one mine to another in Ocampo, in Villa Escobedo, in Durango. The round that made him think that hope and desire always pass us by, always go further from us, because if man were not limited he would never know his destiny, would never see the limits beyond which he cannot go, beyond which he will always fail.

He spent many long vigils in the hospital corridors, in the rooms, in hallways lit by a bulb where a nurse sat behind a table: the odors of medicine, of the sick, the noise and the voices in the other rooms, the relatives of other patients in the hallways, speaking in low voices, smoking. For several days he was ringed in by fatigue, by a lack of sleep, by memories of the sierra, by winter in all the streets of Chihuahua. Every dawn found him with his son. But all happened slowly like a renewal of all things, of all years. The winter and the long walks mixed themselves with the days of that sickness, and the hours filled him with something like a sound, with a heat that made him cry in silence.

"I'm afraid," his son told him one night, from his hospital bed.

Alfredo felt it also, but stifled it with the winter, with fatigue, with the obsession that this couldn't happen to him, to something his. He tried to tell himself that it was not necessary to remain here. But he remembered that he had never left these same sites and territories. It was to flee in a circle, from place to place, always returning to the same thing.

"All of us feel it sometimes, son," he answered. "But we'll go to another place. Here there isn't enough for us. Fear is a passing thing. It's good to know about it so as to understand how to treat it later."

But one morning his son spoke of his grandparents' house, of the afternoons in which he left the school and the railway station when he accompanied his grandfather and they sat on the platforms. Alfredo listened to him say that he liked the smell and seeing the motionless, dirty cars. He also spoke of the silence of the sierra when they arrived at Sánchez and of the Tarahumara girl of Isoguichi.

On the other hand, Alfredo remembered a night in Durango, in the Guadiana Woods, when his son was five years old and became lost among the people gathering branches; he saw his tiny figure disappear in the darkness of the trees. Seconds later Alfredo was running, shaken by an absurd sadness, frightened, beseiged by tears, and he shouted loudly two, perhaps three times, and suddenly he saw his son returning in the distance and caught a wisp of his laughter; Alfredo stopped, watching with relief as he approached, opening his arms; and he felt the tears warring again in his chest, not from fear, but because his son was running toward him out of darkness and silence, as one does to the tormented and resentful arms of life. *Later on children are more complicated than oneself,* said his father, *but it's sweeter embracing them when they're children because it's incomprehensible how life can continue in something so fragile, so defenseless.*

The second week Irene arrived in Chihuahua. The three of them spent the greater part of their time together.

Alfredo began to understand that of all the women with whom he had ever been, she was the only one with whom he could rest, feel footloose, free of life's furies, necessities, and astonishments. But that night he felt the weight of winter, the rarified air of the hospital as a new form of suffocation from cold, from fog, from insomnia; a weight on his shoulders like the arm of a wounded man one drags uselessly for the sole purpose of letting him die in another spot, a few steps further on. He was at the foot of the bed; what he saw in Irene's face were dry lips, eyes reddened from lack of sleep, hair collected at the back of the neck. He felt the dryness in his mouth, but beneath that a painful emptiness, as though his tongue were a metal claw which followed a wayward scent, pierced it and made the smell of medicines, the bitterness of his saliva insipid by comparison. His son died before his eyes as if he only wanted to sleep, worn out by the fever. Far away, exceptionally far, he heard the moaning of his wife, the hoarse and uncontrollable voice of his wife, the movements of the nurse, the doctor's steps, the coldness of the brass bed, the fire that was burning his face, his eyes, staining with water the brightness of all that he saw. On his back Alfredo felt the breath and the hands of all his days mixed together, like another life for his fatigue in another confused brain, in another time beyond repair, another regret that remained between his hands like so much dust. He remembered a morning as a boy when he accompanied his father to the services at the Methodist Church; and, while the winter wind fluttered his overcoat and lifted his scarf, the pastor said that hope exists when there is no faith because faith is the certainty and hope the desire to have that certainty, the desire that faith should really exist.

Irene left Chihuahua two days later, but Alfredo remained there. He would return to Estación Creel; he would once more take up the work of looking for deposits, but without the help of friends, alone. He would continue in this way for four years, little by little losing money, insisting he didn't know whether he or the sierra were the cause, if his purpose were to make a killing or to find protection in an impregnable refuge, in spite of the uselessness, of the fact his other children would separate themselves from him like the last fragments of metal in an abandoned shaft—all this with a weight of fatigue that is not human, but without any desire to leave, simply understanding, separating himself from everything.

"Irene," he said, on taking leave of her that night in the bus station, "I need to explain things to you better than I have. We've only talked about the mines and the lack of money. I can't say what you have lived through with me, you know. Now I feel that I can't own anything, that work is more than you and I. I want to be able to do anything, to lose or get back everything. But realize, Irene, my son didn't die because of me; he didn't die because he stayed with me."

He examined a vein, a gray vein, or reddish, or white, a vein that on being touched arrested the days and the cities and the dreams and let him hear the noise of a river far below the surface, deeper than his memory or forgetfulness, in the depths of the sierra where the Tarahumara names gave the sensation of being the first names of all things, where the settlements, the rivers, the unspannable gorges were the same as the names, primitive and untouchable, inviolate, and the harshly accented words were like fragments of fallen rock, each syllable like a fruit of the sierra, of time, in the mouth. Several times Alfredo was among groups of the local natives who one morning would begin something which they would not finish until days later: the footrace by men and women after a hard ball that was rolled tirelessly around the village, between fires, the corn liquor, the bets, the cries. One night he conversed with drunken, laughing Tarahumaras while the summer beat against his brain, together with the dense but intermittent voices of the game. There, drunk at the festival of Carichi, he felt himself cry, carry his hands to his eyes and cry without restraint, but without pain, without hopelessness, as if it were his turn in the wheel of days to cry without sadness or anguish; he got up and under the influence of hours of drinking passed numerous fires, shouts, Indians drunk or sleeping on the ground, wiping his tears like a labor, like an obligation imposed by time or by his insensitivity; and next to some huts he stopped and then cried with pain, hearing the impersonal round of his days like an embrace of the sierra, like the shouts and laughter he didn't understand; and his body was a fading memory, a bitter and tired burden in search of another place, or another understanding. He wept while an avalanche of minerals, of nights, of stars, of fatigue fell over him, burying him in the dream, yanking him from the mine, the mine he had never found, save in the confused ground of his hope, in a will that was broken and solitary, scattered from breath-taking precipices in the paternal body of the sierra and of summer, in the festival of the entrails of dismembered bulls, in the laughter, the shouts among the fires, while he fought to overcome his implacable fatigue.

The Present
IV

"Hey, kid, come here," said Alfredo, sitting at the table, opening a bottle of Dorado brandy. "We are going to celebrate with my family. Irene! Come here, bring your two daughters over here. Irene!" he said, while he poured brandy in glasses for everyone. "Where's my son-in-law? Shit, where is Raúl? I want to speak with him! To tell him he's rich now, that he's going to eat out of my hand for the rest of his life."

Irene came closer, but without sitting down at the table. Speaking under her breath in a voice that was cold and abrupt, she tried to restrain him.

"Where is Raúl?" Alfredo said again. "I want to clarify several points with him. Not with you, Irene. I want to tell him who will maintain this house, understand?"

"That's enough, Dad," said his oldest daughter. "Don't start in with the same insults as always. That's enough."

"Leave him alone, Isabel," intervened Irene. "Leave him alone. Don't you start up now."

"I can't stand it when he comes home like this. What has he been working at so hard?" replied Isabel. "Is working hard letting Raúl support us all?"

"Drink, Jesús," said Alfredo. "Drink Julia's glass. I'll

drink Irene's. Go ahead, drink." Alfredo finished his cup slowly; then he turned toward them. "Listen to me. I want to speak with Raúl. I don't want to leave this house without talking to him, without telling him he's going to eat out of my hand all the rest of his life, him and you, Isabel, and everyone. I want to tell him that. Do you hear? Jesús, wait"—the boy had gotten up from the table to leave the house, already feeling the alcohol working in his brain. "Hold on, we'll leave together in a moment. I can't stand their complaints anymore. First your father, later Pastor Ramírez, now Raúl. I'm fed up with sermons. None of them has been as much of a man as I have. None of them has a strength equal to mine. They're incapable of fighting for a piece of glass. I have lifted myself out of misery. I have bettered myself in spite of everyone: partners and children and family. In spite of misery and mistrust. There has always been mistrust. I have made my life alone. Yes, and everyone, even after my death is going to be eating because of me, you and your children . . . Now, get out of here. Go! Leave this room so we can be alone. We want to celebrate by ourselves. Get out of here. Did you hear? And warn Raúl. Tell him yourself, Irene. Do you understand?"

Alfredo's face was red, his eyes suffused with blood to the point of bursting. His respiration was violent, agitated, and his mouth was marked by an uneven smile that was tense, bitter. While he remained on his feet, looking toward the window, his daughters and Irene left the dining room. He continued to stand there, looking at the closed window, with its yellow curtains. Then he sat down. He filled two glasses and told the boy to sit down and drink with him, to celebrate the evening. The boy thought about Ana, and suddenly he forgot everything he'd heard: the trip, Alfredo, the house, and only the image of Ana showed itself, brilliant and pure in his memory, in his being. Alfredo got up with difficulty. Then he remained standing next to the table, looking at the woven tablecloth, the empty glasses.

"Take the cigarettes, kid, there on the table. Let's go drink somewhere else. I'm tired of this place."

Alfredo buttoned his shirt carefully. He breathed deeply. There was a bitterness in his mouth, a fatigue. He placed his hands on a chest of drawers; he caressed the wood. He saw the old walls, the pictures of his children, the Last Supper, a calendar.

"Let's go, kid. The devil take this place. There's nothing to drink here."

They opened the door. The dark street was lit by a weak bulb next to the brick wall by the orchard. They went up the street toward the avenue called Quintas. It was fully night now. The sensation of being in Parral again made them feel the village was a house in which they had been placed, protected from everything, from every fate, from every dream, from every failure. There were many people seated outside their houses on account of the summer's heat. They walked more quickly, with a fury in their souls that made them laugh and say the first thing that came to mind, to want everything at once. A euphoria grew in the boy as if desperation had turned into a spur to laughter, to volubility. He wanted to hurry back to Ana, to be in the village, to feel himself lost. *Ana,* he said to himself, *Ana.* And her image dissolved in the laughter of the night, in the nascent drunkenness, the novelty. The lighted part of the street ended; they lowered their voices as if the street might hear them. They went through the stable gates; the corrals gave off an odor of pasture, of animals, of gunny sacks, of iron. A trailer was at the end, without wheels, supported by wooden blocks. From there could be seen the silhouette of the dry river bed, the bushes on both sides, like fistfuls of miniaturized dwellings. A full moon rose in the sky, becoming steadily whiter and stronger. The boy remembered the nights in Talamantes, the innumerable stars which seemed on the point of falling, the rumor of the distant river. The nights in which he ran, trying to arrive at Talamantes de Arriba ahead of his fear. There was a lot of loose dust. As they got closer, they could see people through the lit windows. They entered El Suchiate. There were few people at that hour. They took a table near the musicians' stage, which was empty at the moment, passing only one occupied table en route.

The boy felt how the intoxication rose slowly through his body, through his brain, through his movements. His mouth was thick, the saliva insipid and bitter at the same time. And he also felt euphoria, the welcome spread of pleasure, of laughter, the absence of precise memories, save those of feeling powerful, of being lifted to the tops of trees, of mountains by the florescence of silver.

"But it's Amelia I'm thinking about, Alfredo . . . I swear to you it's only her I love. I swear it," said the boy. "Ever since I was a boy I've thought about marrying her. I'm going to go, yes, for God's sake . . ."

The boy made a gesture with his hands, as if wishing that Alfredo would quiet down, would not insist. Alfredo saw him euphoric, drunk already. They drank the brandy slowly, as if with each sip they saw life more clearly, the luminous destiny of life, the route of their destiny without rocks to trip them, without walls, without stain.

"It's more important for me to go to Talamantes," the boy repeated. "To tell my father and my brothers about this. I'll take them away from there, yes. Let them sell my father's land and come with me. Let them know that Jesús González is the best in Talamantes."

Alfredo answered scornfully, but stopping short of denial, as if certain facts were accepted by both of them.

"I will open the mine, you understand, not you, kid," Alfredo began. "You will live like a parasite off the mine. You will live well, I know. You will learn to live well because in addition to the rest you've learned, you'll have to learn even that . . ."

He spoke to him with a contempt that became brighter again, and little by little took root in the night. *But he never will understand the mine as I do, Armando. The man who only works for ASARCO as a peon can't know what a mine is, no; he can't know what it is to have it in his dreams for years, what it is to wrest it from life, to make it all happen.* But I knew that scorn was also an expression of humiliation. Hours later he would make me realize that he felt it several times, not only that night. It was the humiliation of seeing himself after all these years in the company of that boy, of a farmer who worked in the mine. It was a kind of naked resentment against life's weight, against his failures without buffering; everything had been let loose against him in a way that was plain for all to see. They had already drunk two glasses of brandy in that place and were about to receive a third. Alfredo was tired, even a bit sleepy. But he was calm, a momentary calm. He ran his hand through his hair, among the dirty, disordered locks. The boy continued talking without Alfredo's hearing him. But now he saw how the boy's eyes grew smaller and more irritated with drink. He saw the boy clumsily lighting a cigarette, as if he didn't know how to manage his hands, as though he'd never smoked before. Alfredo looked around the place. He saw that the number of people had increased, that they had filled the tables, that the cigarette smoke, the laughter, the voices, the music covered them.

"Look, Jesús, pay attention to what I am going to tell you. Special attention. Listen carefully," said Alfredo. "I know them. They won't be long in looking for us. Maybe this very day, or tomorrow, or next week. But they'll come looking for us, do you understand? This is important . . . Because it has to do with my work, with something I've done and have to do . . ."

Alfredo observed the change in the boy's face, the dark forehead beaded with sweat, with dust, filthy; his thick lips expelling a foul alcoholic breath that mouthfuls of smoke did not dissipate. Alfredo spoke with clarity, but also with haste, anguish, rancor. He restrained himself from shouting, from bragging about the mine before all the other tables, from shouting that he didn't want to support anyone or anything again.

"I have to do it, kid," Alfredo repeated. "I have waited many years. I've always wanted a vein like this, not as a beginning, no, not as a beginning . . . I want this kind of finish, for things to end well . . . They'll find where we are, do you understand? But it has to do with something more important than them. And than their property. It has to do with what I've done and what I have to do. With what I am. We are going to reach an agreement. We have to form a company . . . No, you don't understand this, Jesús . . . I have to open that mine. Get this through your head. I have to put it in operation, whatever the cost. And to do that we need the owners of the land to form a company with us or sell us their land or give us permission to work there. They could buy the machinery, or whatever, and we could do the work. All my life I have known how to work. But we have to speak with them, Jesús . . . I, therefore, must speak with them. They have to accept us. With don Enrique, principally. Because he will make the others agree . . . They will look for us, but I have to speak beforehand with him. I have to locate him. Do you understand, Jesús? Remember this well because it's what matters. Tomorrow, no later than tomorrow . . . Today we celebrate. This night is for celebration, but tomorrow, before they look for us, we ought to do it . . . But today we celebrate, understand? Today we celebrate," said Alfredo, and then drank from his glass.

The boy did the same, making the twisted smile of a drunkard, lacking in sense now, with the muscles of his face sagging as though he had received a dose of sedatives. Alfredo left his glass on the table. He looked around the brothel, which seemed brimming with music, voices, laughter, women. At a nearby table were the same men he had noticed on arriving; one was an old man under a cocked hat revealing only a shock of white hair; another, already drunk, wore a fringed leather jacket and embraced a woman. The third affected a bolo tie and a felt hat with a wide brim, tipped to one side. Alfredo looked at them. He asked for his bill and two more glasses of brandy. When they brought the cups, Alfredo raised his and saluted the other table.

"To your health, gentlemen," said Alfredo, and he took a swallow. The older man turned around to look at him; the other too, with reddened eyes and a wobbly head. Alfredo and the boy moved through the tables and out onto the street, where the warm night air suddenly felt clean, full of crickets, without smoke, without music. They still felt a euphoria, dominated now by drunkenness which became purer, more irresistible as they moved down the street.

The Past
V

During the years that he remained in Parral, a girl was born and later his second son. Afterwards, he left for Guadalupe y Calvo, at the southern end of the Chihuahua sierra, still working for Manuel Robles. Between Nobogamé and Guadalupe y Calvo they explored a silver and lead mine, looking for offshoots of the vein. For several months he was in charge of exploration. The principal vein was good for double shifts by the third year. Alfredo was once again full of his work, which opened a path back into himself, to his pride, to his strength. He insisted on taking charge of everything himself, demanding a share, not just a salary. When the cost of exploiting the vein proved higher than its value, they blamed him for a careless assessment. Robles had to sell the equipment to pay off the debts and Alfredo was fired. When the two of them returned to Parral, Robles did not hire him again in the mine that he continued working near Nieves in Durango, nor for the metal shipments which were bought from gambusinos for the mills. Alfredo nevertheless felt a new liberty which came from cutting his ties with friends, from breaking the train of his many years of work, from all the years that suddenly came together, that fused in his soul with a familiar flavor of rocks, of metal, of men. But it's only a matter of time, thought Alfredo, time that he had to endure until he returned to the same vein that opened in all his memories and desires; it was only a matter of patience, only that, he told himself with joy, with the pride which comes from denying oneself, allowing the weeks to pass, letting life go by in such a way as to gain more strength, to become firmer in his memories. He tasted time going by with dizzying speed, harsh as the man, as he was in his feelings.

Before winter set in, he was back in Parral. The house seemed older to him, full of objects, things collected by his wife. In the month of July, before his return, his eldest daughter had married a Methodist boy, an accountant, and I took his place in the civil and religious ceremonies. Seeing his house, his family made him feel closer to himself, perhaps because he felt he no longer lived with them. The river in Parral was dusty, some parts covered by an ancient scab where no child had ever stepped, only the wind. Everything seemed hazy, as if a smoke of sleep had fallen over life, a dust of years gradually covering the dreamer until it formed him in its own image and likeness. Everything was barren: the hills, the walnut groves, the orchards of Las Quintas. He was jobless for a long time. But for Alfredo it was like getting up again in the midst of the current of his days, hearing the sounds that rose as he passed, a rumor of memories, of thoughts like birds which fly without falling to earth, with the secret pride of being able to conquer or to rebel in the presence of oneself, of one's hopes.

The following year he made occasional trips within the state, hauling cattle, wood, or cement in trucks and trailers belonging to a partnership on Ahumada Street. Alfredo wanted to return to the sierra. He looked for friends who would accompany him; none accepted. He quarreled with Irene because he laid aside money from his trucking hauls against his return to the sierra. Toward October of 1960, his daughter Isabel married and brought her husband to live in the house. Because of the money which his son-in-law contributed from that time on, Alfredo felt justified in keeping all his earnings for himself.

He left for the sierra in 1961 and was gone two years. As a miserable gambusino, he returned once again to his familiar haunts, step after step, river by river, no longer whole nor full of hope, as if the secret inertia which guided him didn't flow from strength, but stubbornness. In the sierra Alfredo experienced obsessive replays of the last afternoons he had spent in Minas Nuevas years earlier. One lonely night he was oppressed by a distant, muffled voice. Because in none of his thoughts had he ever thought he would become old, that old age awaited and would waylay him. For others, yes, it would; we saw it approach us, felt it take us by the arms, the heart. But not he, not Alfredo.

He returned to Parral and remained here a full year. It snowed several times in January. Through the kitchen window he would see the fallen snow, almost violet, at daybreak. Further away the snow accumulated in the river bed, hiding the dust under the cold, under a shadow of calm or a caress of immense fingers. He looked for the boy during the afternoons, hoping to talk about the old mines. He remained for hours in that house, speaking with him and with Ana. She was a woman older than the boy, also of impassive expression. She sat for long periods on the bed or stood looking out the window without noticing Alfredo, without listening, remaining locked in the heat of her flesh, of her body. She served them coffee or at times mezcal, when Alfredo brought it. He left very late; on crossing the first streets he felt the fallen snow more as an enclosure than as the out-of-doors. He still carried the heat in his body, the sensation of being shut in the tiny house, his mouth tired from the mezcal and the cigarettes. The snow burst like the fragments of many years, an old age of the world or of the universe, something pure in the air that appeared during winter and fell on the land, leaving a whiteness that the morning couldn't equal, invading every man with a sudden awareness of another whiteness in himself, in spite of everything.

He had to finish the work he'd been doing, no matter that the old will was more a memory than an actuality. A damaged road, a will-o'-the-wisp which the hands seek, not a life that awakes in a man like the light in a woman's eyes, her hands, or her body. *I can't explain it all because it's bigger than I am, Armando,* he told me that night, *but this is the only way in which I can understand it, the only way.*

The second winter Pastor Ramírez was here for two weeks. Following the end of the Sunday service, Alfredo met with him in the tiny living room of the rectory and they talked about his father, about his life in the sierra, his growing poverty and his stubbornness. Pastor Ramírez seemed worn by age and bewildered at being here and by his efforts to convince Alfredo. At times they remained quiet as if allowing soothing rain to fall over these hours, over their discussion. Several times Alfredo wanted to get up and embrace him, to tell him to forget everything, that nothing they said was important.

"I don't want to sit down in the door of my house and wait for everything to fix itself, Pastor, no," insisted Alfredo. "I know. It's how I've lived and what I taught my son, the reason I won't allow myself to play the coward. If we do, what business have we here?" asked Alfredo. "Who else is there to fight for us?"

For many years Alfredo had known that on this crowded earth there is no family for us, for forgetfulness or the night. The plant grows without a father to feed it; animals grow without a mother to make them happy when they grow old; disorder and violence blossom in everybody without the parents' taking charge of the richness or the misery of our lives. *But obviously not everything is solitude, not everyone is alone nor arrives alone,* Alfredo said to himself, asking who in the world had thrown this old man in front of him, with those useless sentiments that he clung to to go on living, to continue loving.

"I know you don't believe what you're saying, Alfredo," added the pastor. "A man learns very late in life that everything is fraught with risk."

"I clearly remember the Sunday you explained it differently," said Alfredo. "Let the dead bury the dead. Yes, you said that a Christian ought not to worry about how he will live tomorrow, nor how he will dress himself, nor how he will bury his dead, because if the birds go on living, even more should a child of God. Remember? My father was there. You talked about it later . . . I know that when I submit to everyone, Pastor, that when I cease hearing my own life, I am dead, and that way I help everyone I love to die. Life is a kind of absurd dream, very heavy, more than the weight of the dirt in the mine. And to love those near me, to help them to die as I do, is to bury them, to make the dead bury each other. But I feel as injured, as rejected as Irene or any of the others. I can't take them with me in my search, to fail with me."

Alfredo got up, intending to leave. He felt the solidity, the shadowy interior of the house. The pastor detained him.

"Wait, I'll go with you."

They crossed the garden. The grass was dry. At the back, a peach tree remained standing, naked, proof against the wind. They opened the old wooden gate and went out into the sidestreet, moving on toward the corner. Several children played in the Plaza Guillermo Baca. The sky was a solid gray with some faint pink cracks. Alfredo took pleasure in the cold and in the freezing wind that reached them from the sidestreets.

"Do you think you're right, Alfredo?" said the pastor, drawing his overcoat more tightly around him as they crossed the street. Alfredo didn't answer. *All I know is what kills me is not the way, or isn't like the blood or the hands which grow dirty in their work,* Alfredo told himself. *The trees and the dust make no sense; neither do wood or death. We can't understand the world, questioning it with something as fragile as the reason.*

"You forget what gave us life," continued the pastor. "Yes, you forget God, Alfredo. You forget everything you learned in my house, everything I tried to teach you to make you strong, so you wouldn't fall this way."

They had passed through several streets and stopped at

the Guanajuato Bridge. Alfredo looked at the dry bed of the river, at the sky, which was cloudy, opaque, where the night was slowly filtering away. Crossing the bridge were some automobiles, heavily wrapped women, children running. In the background with humble pride dry trees held out naked limbs to the wind which whistled over the bridge.

"Do you know what I like?" said Alfredo. "To feel this frozen wind. To see the skin of my hands, of my back wear away, Pastor. To feel that I sleep in the dirt, that I search in it, that it is far more extensive than we are. To know nothing has to be understood. That it's enough for everyone to ruin himself in the way that seems best. Or that everyone should seize life however he can, however he is able to."

"No, I don't understand you, Alfredo. I only know a man is bound to be unhappy if he doesn't accept his family, if he doesn't accept life. None of us can choose to live with abandon or rage."

"No . . . Wait, Pastor, listen, understand what I'm saying. Irene said many years ago that she loved me. Why? She doesn't know how to love. Neither do you; neither do I. All we want is to solve life blindly, using a feeling . . . Sometimes I want to drop everything and run away in anguish, punished by what I have done or haven't done, and take refuge in my daughters, in Irene, in Irene's bed, in the food that Irene makes . . . But I love my children; I loved my son to the point of anguish and sorrow, Pastor."

"I feel sorry for you, Alfredo," said the pastor, looking about for some way to avoid the wind which was fluttering his overcoat. "Love is not fury. One loves existence, life,

Alfredo. You're not afraid to step on feelings which get in your way. You've reached the point where you feel neither happiness nor misfortune. You're finished. It's not a challenge, but your cowardice, your failure. God doesn't deliver us to a destiny so blind and egotistical."

From the bridge Alfredo stared off into the distance, at the pinnacles in the suburb of Topo Chico. A tall tenement stood out amidst the trash, the rocks, and the cloudy sky. *Soon it will snow,* thought Alfredo; *in a few days it will begin to snow.* He observed the leafless cottonwoods on the other side; then he looked toward the far end of the bridge, toward the Plaza Juárez. The wind increased. Alfredo felt that, yes, it's true, nobody is pushed into a destiny because destiny is oneself, an anxiety to conquer or comprehend. *I have no wish to kill myself,* Alfredo thought, *but to let time pass, to see how things turn out, the things I have done. To do so is harder than repenting everything I have done, as if not until now could I raise my eyes and know the peace of total being, without having to drink the years in sips bitter as sweat, as fatigue, as the money I never had.* The wind grew stronger. The day began to darken, the night falling from the cloudy sky on the houses, on the pastor who had drawn his scarf to the level of his mouth. The gleam of the old eyes could barely be seen, appearing like a last glint of light among the embers of the memories of Alfredo's infancy, which had formed so many winters ago. Once more Alfredo wanted to embrace him, to tell this old man he would take care of him always, that he didn't want to see him alone in the cold, lost in the distance winter breeds; that he should go back, return to the church.

"Yes, my life is a failure," he replied. "But it's been sincere, Pastor, and I feel I've had the worst of it, that things haven't gone as I wished, and I don't know where I got off the track. Afterwards, when I accepted what I was and that life would never be the way I wanted it, Pastor, I asked myself if anything had any value or was worth the price, if a life is really a life. Because it's not just circumstances that bring about the failure, you understand, but yourself. I resisted the necessity of seeing just how far I was lost; even now I feel like a stranger, the man who lived in my place, who lived my days, who loved Irene, who ate my food. It's like being in the sierra, Pastor, like weeping in the sierra without a woman for months which seem like iron seeds in the soul, in sleep, in your tired blood. And Parral blankets me with these streets, with these people, with this feeling that time has passed more rapidly than I have advanced and won't go slower, won't wait for me; and finally it stops as if challenging me, ceases to run as I have run, as I have lived."

Alfredo walked all afternoon the following day, feeling the frozen wind in his face, on his body. The sky was cloudy; a gray cape, sometimes tinged with rose, spread into the night, promising another snowstorm. He returned to his house very late at night. He found Irene awake, sewing next to the woodstove. Alfredo looked around for something to eat. He heated beans and meat in a frying pan and prepared a cup of black coffee. After eating, he sat down next to her, smoking in silence for several minutes. At the end of an hour Alfredo watched her get up and begin to put away her sewing.

"Wait . . ." Alfredo said to her. "Wait, Irene. I want to talk with you, to chat a minute."

Irene went on putting away her sewing. When she was through, she turned toward him, waiting for him to speak. Alfredo saw her tired eyes, the white in her hair.

"I spoke with Pastor Ramírez . . ." he began.

Irene did not respond. She continued looking at him, waiting. Alfredo experienced a certain anxiety. He was more aware of the silence of the house, of the odor of wood burning in the stove. Then he got up, searched out some sticks of wood and put them in the stove. Afterwards he sat down again in front of her.

"I spoke with Pastor Ramírez," he said again. "He's old now, much aged . . . I wonder if he really believes what he said. If in truth a man can live that way."

"Is that all?" asked Irene.

"I've also been thinking other things, Irene. For example, that it's strange we don't know the moment in which we change . . . Now I know that life is more complex. Death also. I haven't ceased believing in God, for example, but in His simplicity. Because I really haven't ceased believing in life, Irene, no, only in its simplicity, its purity. But I believed that you were strong, that nothing could tire you . . . We can't feel the same, no. For me, our relationship has ended because you lacked the strength to follow me in my work; for you, we have ended because I was not up to my work, because I was weak in taking charge of life."

Irene listened to him. Alfredo turned toward her, searching her eyes as he watched her get up. She returned his glance without changing expression.

"Yes, that's the way it is," said Irene, in a voice that was open and mild. "That's the way it is, Alfredo," she repeated.

The Present
V

I saw them when they entered El Flamingo. Alfredo wore a denim jacket, an old hat tipped to one side, and clothes that were filthy with dirt. They were already moving among the tables when I reached them. Alfredo looked at me, surprised. He had on muddy miner's boots the same as the boy. He hugged me, striking me hard on the back, rasping my face with several days' growth of beard that was already turning white and partially hid his tired face, his open mouth. The boy's smile was half grimace, and he had a sweaty face; in one hand he held a cigarette in the manner of farmers, gripping it with two fingers while leaving the rest of the hand completely open. He smiled at me, exposing a row of large teeth that were encrusted with tartar. Then he let out a small laugh, soft, a mixture of pride and timidity, of boastfulness. I conducted them to the table where we had been for several hours. Alfredo greeted everyone. Robles bought them a round. Alfredo smiled; he threw back his head and gave forth a peal of laughter.

"Armando," he said, in a loud voice, "tell your friends that when I'm here, I pay. Say it, shit, so they understand. Let them celebrate with me; it's so they can celebrate with me."

The boy was still on his feet, but reeling, holding the burnt-out cigarette in his hand. He tried to approach me and draw out a chair. Alfredo was inordinately boastful about the vein. Manuel Robles was delighted; Alfredo didn't realize that they listened without believing him. Robles and Alfredo appeared almost identical: tall, blond, with green eyes and faces reddened by drink and the heat.

"He was your friend, wasn't he?" Manuel Robles repeated, reinitiating the conversation that we had been carrying on at the table before Alfredo's arrival. "They killed him because he didn't want to pay on time. There was a lot of money involved, it seems."

"No, he was no friend of Alfredo's," said Saúl.

Alfredo leaned toward me, asking for a cigarette. José María, who had joined us, supplied him. Alfredo took the pack and with difficulty got one out. I saw him relax, feel a moment of calm, of satisfaction.

"It depends on who you want to see, Alfredo. That's what friends are for," insisted Manuel Robles. "I'll help you, I already told you. You weren't so distrustful when we worked together."

I saw that the boy was tired, bathed in a friendly heat that was his alone, that surrounded his sweaty, drunken solitude. When Alfredo answered that he needed to see don Enrique, Robles sprawled in his seat and took a sip from his glass. Then he smiled and said to me:

"What's your opinion, professor? I think our friend here has problems."

I know that Alfredo felt a rebirth of the scorn, the ire, the pain he had felt many years earlier when Manuel Robles had denied him money and had hired another, less qualified, man in his place. Once more there was mockery in Robles's reddened face, also scorn. Alfredo was bragging about what he could do without his help. He wanted to recover the power of being more, of being enough in himself.

"Why do you want to see don Enrique?" asked Robles. "The old man is not in Parral, he's in Chihuahua City . . . He only comes here rarely. Let me know exactly what's going on so I can help you," he added.

"It's true he comes here seldom," I added.

"I'm thirsty," answered Alfredo, after a long pause. "I want beer. I want to drink something cold."

I didn't understand him then, only hours later. At that time I had only a confused sense of his interest in don Enrique. He was in a hurry, yes, but a hurry greater than seemed necessary to file a claim. He wanted to bring everything to a head and make things turn out right. He wanted to throw off the stupor and open himself to easy laughter, to conversation, to the resentment which flowed like sweat from his face.

"Don Enrique didn't want Rafael to be municipal president," Robles commented to Alfredo. "Villela came out, as you see. Tell Alfredo the whole thing," Robles said to me. "Tell him how they named the governor in Chihuahua. Go ahead."

"Please, not Armando," Saúl broke in. "Let Lalo tell him. Poets take too long. Anyone but Armando."

"The governor asked him to call," said José María, "to reach an accord with don Enrique about the nomination. Carlos reminded him that the municipal presidency was not his business, but everyone's. But they say that the governor allowed them to strip Rafael of the presidency on account of that meeting, out of respect for the opinion of don Enrique. Rafael was a little lacking in courage."

"Without balls, don't you think, Alfredo?" said Robles. "Like the way you and I used to work. Are you listening? It's necessary to work on equal terms, with respect for the opinions of friends, not only for our own."

Then I saw it, seconds later, when Saúl was already pushing at the boy and everyone laughed at his antics. Without realizing it, I also rose from the table. From very far away, as if from the distant tranquility of a dream, the boy went down amidst the dizzying laughter, under the hot breath of Saúl, who was shaking him. The boy felt himself fall under the tables, under our feet, where he looked for us with his eyes and continued to defend himself more to make Saúl stop laughing and his breath go away than to halt the insults, to stop the fists. When I intervened, Saúl had fallen over another table, thrown there by the boy.

"Let me go, Armando," Saúl shouted at me. "Let me go, I tell you!"

Everyone at the table was looking at us. I felt Manuel Robles's eyes on me. I also saw they were looking at Alfredo. But Alfredo was occupied with his own thoughts, without paying attention to what we were saying at the table, forgetting even the resentment he used to feel for Robles. He looked at us as if we had all been cast aside on the stony earth, covered with dust, without rhyme or reason, direction or tools. In his eyes the rivers ran, carrying the corrosive odor of memories, of all mankind. Saúl laughed with difficulty, resentfully. It was then I released him. The boy drank the beer they had brought him; he didn't realize right away, until several fresh, bitter swallows later, that they were speaking to him.

"Defend him again," said Robles, irritated. "Let the little professor defend him again."

Alfredo bowed in his seat. A heavy sweat slid down his cheeks, down his neck. I saw brilliant drops of sweat on the backs of his hands. He spit on the floor. His mouth no doubt felt hot, his saliva thick owing to the bitterness of the beer. He lowered his head slowly, feeling a peace in his neck, in his shoulders. He looked at the floor, covered with cigarettes, matches, gobs of spit; he saw our black city shoes, also the boy's boots. In his eyes I saw a small light of intense life, in spite of his intoxication. He reached out an arm to me, paying attention to no one else at the table. But then he turned toward Robles, remembering their recent conversation.

"Rafael is my friend, I warn you," he said. "I don't give a shit if you people weren't able to keep City Hall for yourselves."

"They've stood you free drinks a few times because you were at his table, not because of friendship, Alfredo," replied Robles. "He never has helped you. You're mixing up your friends."

Alfredo looked at me again while he took two wrinkled bills from his pants pocket. The slight rhythmic swaying of his head was evidence of the drunkenness which had overtaken him.

"That's the reason I'm going to pay for what I have drunk," he said, slowly. "Armando, you take this and pay what Jesús and I owe. What's left over can pay for some drinks for them . . . And now I'm leaving this table. I'm in a hurry. I've already lost much time with him, many years."

"Come here, Alfredo!" shouted Robles. "Tell us about the mine, you mistrustful old man. I'll tell you where you can get rich!"

I got up, too, to follow them. I wanted to leave them in a spot well away from the others. I was aware of the tables brushing against me, of the noise of the brothel, palpable like a body, like something I could touch. We found a table on the opposite side of the room. The boy sat down and once more a wave of sleep rolled over him. His face and his back were sweaty. Sleep set him apart from the noise, sliding along his arms and down his neck. Suddenly he straightened himself and began insulting Alfredo; when he looked at us, we saw his burnt-out eyes like wet ash that doesn't lose its clarity and shines with a faint light, like old water, like water about to evaporate. He wanted to knock Alfredo down, to insult him; but Alfredo remained quiet, uninterested. There was a lot of noise. Alfredo's flushed face with its grizzled beard shadowing his cheeks, his neck, showed he was now wide awake, on the edge of mockery, of laughter. I don't know how much time had passed when I saw Alfredo's hand pressing the boy's. The boy wanted to withdraw his hand, but Alfredo pressed it all the harder. I saw the wrist slip from underneath the fingers, as from many straps of fire which had ignited in the skin, while the boy's reddened fists remained separated on the table top. Alfredo finished his beer and left the bottle on the table. He wanted a woman; he needed a woman. I thought about going, of leaving them this way.

When Alfredo went off to a room, the boy became nauseous at the taste of beer; he spat on the floor and ran the back of his hand over his mouth. He felt tired, as if he carried many things within himself, many thoughts that mixed themselves together and also a persistent voice which he failed to identify, in spite of the hand that was also there, on his shoulder. Chema spoke to him again, and the boy glanced up; across all the voices in his head, all the fatigue, the noise, he heard himself being invited back again to Robles's table. He got up without answering, or perhaps saying something, because I saw Chema smile, agreeing. When we arrived at the table, they insisted that the boy have a drink. But he was tired. He said nothing about the mine, although everyone asked him about it. His eyes closed. He said there was a lot of noise. Then he looked at me, as if he were trying to recognize me. Far, very far away, the boy saw Robles watching him. All of a sudden he spoke of his woman; his anguish grew at remaining among us. Then he turned quiet, as though he were not here. As he dozed, one could imagine he was invaded by a grander silence, like the nights in which he awoke before dawn and sensed the warm earth, the hot ashes of the fire. He opened his eyes, but I don't believe he knew he opened them or that he was looking at us. He took his time in returning to the heat of the brothel, in noticing the smoke from cigarettes, the ceiling lights, the men, in hearing the noise of glasses, cries, laughter. All at once he appeared to be in a quiet place, empty, then to wake next to the mine, forgetting the noise of the brothel in which he opened his eyes again. He heard a laugh near him; he heard it again and sat up slightly to see what it was. Saúl was again at his side, laughing. The boy was not interested in what he was saying, but once more he was aware of Saúl's breathing. I saw the others restrain Saúl. I had no desire to get up or involve myself.

"Don't bother him anymore! Quit it!" shouted Robles, who looked at me again.

I saw the boy was thinking about doing something, that inside his dream, his fatigue, in the heat there in front of Saúl, he wanted to do something well, to rise, to strike out, but he only appeared more abandoned, useless.

"Let him say that to me again!" cried Saúl, amidst the movement of men who held him against the table. The boy got up unsteadily. He took a few steps toward the door. His body seemed to grow heavy. Some tables further along I saw him stop. He turned toward us; for several minutes he searched our faces with his eyes.

"Is something wrong, kid?" I asked, when I came up to him. I realized he hadn't moved, that he was far away, that he hadn't taken a step, that we were five tables from the others.

"No, nothing's wrong. I only want to know if you want to fuck your mother."

"Go on, kid. It's all right. No more questions. I don't understand you."

"No, no, shit. Tell me that you're going to fuck your mother. Tell the others to fuck your mother."

Time passed and he continued standing in front of me, sweat running down his back, down his face. His arms were hanging by his sides, motionless. He still felt humiliated. I began to lead him. A tall man with a bolo tie was speaking with Alfredo. The boy arrived at the table and leaned against a chair, looking at the man, searching for a beer or a cigarette as if he had been walking for hours on end, months.

"Get out of here; I told you to go see your whore! Get going!" shouted Alfredo, with a different face, angrily. The other man left, passing near me. Alfredo looked with scorn at the boy, who appeared not to know that we had sat down; his hair was dirty, his face sweaty, his eyes red. The boy looked at Alfredo as though he were not standing in front of him, or even here, but at a great distance, in another time.

"Sons of the living bitch," said Alfredo. "Sons of your whore mother."

Alfredo wanted to insult the boy, but desisted for a moment, closing his eyes. And it was as though he were full, a brimming well in which the water comes to the top and spills over. On closing his eyes, Alfredo felt his entire life oppressing him, the darkness, the plethora of memories, of years and many voices, his, others', many different voices but all his, like the sweat which sprang from him, or like his breathing imbued with the same force, the same tension. When I returned to Robles's table, when unfortunately I left them there, I know that Alfredo felt himself to be in the midst of all the voices that filled him and of all the roads that surfaced and were lost and carried him back to himself like another drunkenness, like another multitude.

"I'm not here for that reason, Andrés. I'm not interested in working with them. I'll go further, more to the north."

"Yes, I understand. But you also might be mistaken. You've always been wrong."

"More to the north, old man. I'll leave Veta Grande to you, I told you."

They stopped in front of the door of the shop. Alfredo continued holding the empty bottle in his hand. He listened to the sounds of the heat around him, to the suffocation of the earth of the abandoned town.

"Yes, I understand," said the old man. "I understand, although I find it a little hard."

They went into the shop. The men were talking with the boy. One of the little boys began to sprinkle the earthen floor from a bucket of water. Alfredo ordered beer. They both drank slowly, savoring the warm bitterness of the beers. The brilliant gray eyes of the old man had grown very small.

"This boy is going with you? . . . You don't know this area, right? No, of course not. Let me tell you. Alfredo and I knew this town in better times. Much better, yes . . ."

The boy listened to the old man, who was leaning on the counter next to Alfredo. He saw the enormous, bony hands which had remained in the village, surviving the silent fall of the houses. He was flattered to be included, to be taken into the conversation. The boy smelled the ancient odor of that body. *(But mining is like this. You have to fight hard, to be filled with desire. Look, it's not a matter of breaking up stones, no. I'm not going to fool you by saying that here you have to have patience. It's easier to plant crops, although certainly not here. The mines are flooded. There are still important deposits, not just for a few years, no. Up there, where you came from, a new shaft has been started. Some of us who live here work there. It would be easier to say it's finished and done with and move on. There are about twenty families. Some still come to shoot up the town; they pass in small trucks. Didn't you notice there are a lot of ranches around here? Look, that is the road. It would be easier for everyone to quit and there would be no one in this place. Yes, I am old, but now you'll find out. A person grows set in his ways, as I have, and continues in this village. It's as if they killed your family and you haven't found out what became of them. Yes, it's something like that. And then of course I worked in the mines. But we weren't like those in Santa Bárbara, and the watchmen of the Tecolote Company viewed us as beasts. Then, in 1932, they broke the miners who joined the union, and one night a body of armed watchmen threatened to kill twenty poor gambusinos and took all their belongings away, even their carbide lamps, and they weren't even on company property. And that continued for a whole year. Because of that they ambushed the head Tecolote watchman and killed him. But not us, no; we didn't do it that way. But you see, in 1929 Veta Grande closed and more than 1,500 miners were without work. The North Americans got permission from Mexico City. Yes, our government arranged for the entire town to be brought to its knees. Mr. Lees claimed it was because of the dam at Boquilla, that the Conchos River didn't supply the dam with enough water to make electricity. Many miners came forward to ask for reparations, and people came from Parral to testify as to the conditions. Poor Mr. Lees was frightened. But that same day, when he came out after speaking with the municipal president, the miners surrounded Mr. Lees in the plaza. Look, right there. Nothing happened to him, but they sent for troops anyway. But in two or three days families were begging for food in the streets. Only we miners who had work helped them. Look, they didn't have enough money to go off and look for work in other places. But they also fired miners in Santa Bárbara, and in San Francisco del Oro and in Parral. At the end of a week I saw how the families would leave, carrying bundles of rags as they went out of town, just like that, without anywhere to go. And that's when it began to snow. And I like to see everything white. I never get tired of seeing everything covered with snow. But that year the cold hurt. It was not snow that was needed right then, when you saw groups of parents and children on foot, dragging bundles of rags along the road. It was rumored that in the Ojinaga area some Gringos had staked other silver claims. Families and boys headed toward that region. But the miners who were Indians died of hunger in the streets, covered with cold and with no idea why work had ceased. But no one paid any attention to action groups, to marches through streets full of snow nor to destitute families. In a short time this town was a changed place, its streets and its little plazas. But the Gringos closed the mines and the town was finished. The remaining families left, the merchants, the miners, and the Gringos left too, taking everything with them. Machinery, tracks, crossties. They didn't forget even a screwdriver. Yes, the Gringos closed the mines and everything was finished. But they're good people. They are good people, sons of bitches. They left the mines flooded. The only thing worse would have been for them to come back again and open the mines and not have anyone say a word against it. Look, it's because my brother had a house here. That's why I stayed. If I could have gone with them to Parral, or to Santa Bárbara, also to Delicias, then yes, I would have done it. But also Mr. Lees spoke to me before going to Cieneguillas. He told me he had a good regard for me and wanted me to work somewhere else. And look, I remembered that conversation for a long time. Still do, yes. It was one afternoon, but near the railway station that was already being dismantled. Mr. Lees had Enrique, a boy who helped him in everything, call me. And I went with him, walking. 'Here I am, Mr. Lees,' I said, when I arrived. Then he spoke to me, smilingly, pushing his hat back and arranging his glasses. 'Now you have nothing to do here,' and I saw a number of men who were taking things down and loading trucks with machinery and equipment, and further below I felt the silence of the village and the cemetery there at my feet, containing more people than the town itself. They were saying goodbye to their dead and leaving the graves more or less arranged, and I looked at the closed houses, the long streets, broken and very lonely. 'Where do you want to go? To Cieneguillas I can't take you, but to Parral or to Santa Bárbara I can. You tell me.' Then I remembered the abuses, the attacks against the gambusinos, the way they only cared about the mines, the persecution of the union members, and the lay-offs, the hungry families, all that they had asked me to do, which pained me now. Enrique came to tell him something and Mr. Lees withdrew. But soon he was back and asked me again, smiling. 'You tell me.' I said to him: 'My brothers have already invited me to go with them. But I told them that I would stay. Look, Mr. Lees, I'll take care of these mines, not for you, but because we are going to work here,' and I already knew I wouldn't, that it would be impossible to work them, that the cooperative wouldn't turn out well, that it wouldn't happen, 'because we are going to work what's here. Yes, Mr. Lees, we have more balls than you and the government. The hunger we know is not going to kill this town; Villa is going to continue. Why did you want to kill gambusinos and prevent them from taking anything from the mines? You don't want us to pick up a single stone. And now you leave the mines flooded. No, Mr. Lees, you take the mines away from us and close Veta Grande for lack of water in the Conchos River, of all things. I know that the drought does not matter to you. You don't want so many miners on the streets, dead of hunger and causing problems throughout the state. Cut off the water and we can go fuck ourselves. I'm staying here. Look, let everyone who leaves go to the devil, and you too, Mr. Lees.')*

"Throughout this entire area there are minerals," said Alfredo. "All you have to do is look for them; you have to know how to work, old man, certainly. But further away. Not here."

The metal in those areas seemed to concentrate in the south of the State of Chihuahua and the north of Durango, as if a mineral heart had taken root there. Now, on his return, Alfredo felt another road drawing near, the door that hadn't opened in the previous thirty years, but had remained in the same place, waiting for him to find it. He found the town abandoned in the same way a man finds forgetfulness or disorder in his soul, while the lives of his wife and children go on rotting, or his very own, slowly. *A man is not the product of his days,* he thought, *although pain is found there, although the pastor says that life is withered by resentment. Although life floods other ruins and forgotten deposits in the dry soil of the soul, always subject to precarious memory and never sufficient in itself.*

They left the shop. Andrés accompanied them on foot beyond the ruins of City Hall, followed by children. The noise of the earth reached off in every direction. Alfredo crossed Minas Nuevas again with the remains of a memory, the life of a man who hasn't managed to disappear at the same time as the places he's been. Sunken like a thought behind him, he left the village in ruins, an abandonment of himself, like a self-prophecy. Suddenly he discovered that a life is more vast than he had believed, that there is room in it to keep things and to forget, to erase the years, people, places, feelings, to leave them submerged as if under much dusty sediment which accumulates in ourselves in order not to hear them when we step on them again, in order that they don't flower when we return to them, because they have been allowed to sink in the years or in an abandoned village, in a ruins that is all-powerful, timeless.

At the end of July they found the vein. It was silver. It was a deep vein that could be followed along a wall for several meters and then sunk itself in the rock, taking the form of a tree. Alfredo thought they would be able to follow it with an inclined shaft. They spent three days in exploration, mapping the strata and collecting samples. They slept very little. The moment they closed their eyes disordered dreams began, filled with a multitude of incoherent, unknown places. The last night seemed endless, charged with so many stars they seemed deafening. A pulsation rose in the earth, in the rocks, in the hills, keeping time with the circulation of the blood. Alfredo placed his hands on the earth and heard a current, a pulse, as if it were full of arteries and a dry blood ran below—thirsty, warm, mineralized. He arranged the saddlebags and harnessed the animals. When this was done, he only took time to heat coffee. For the first time Alfredo noticed the boy was tired. Soon he slept and Alfredo found himself alone next to the fire. Right up to that night, all his dreams, his memories, his life, came back to him. A sense of power invaded him, a feeling of security throughout his body, a serenity he had desired for a long time, since the mines and the mining camp in Durango. But together with the vein, with the silver that blossomed forth again, were these lands. *My God,* thought Alfredo, as he took a handful of dust, tossing it carelessly from him, *why do we always come back to the same thing? Why does it always end this way?* The vein was a seam with offshoots, located in cattle country. Staking the claim, speaking with his old partners, with don Enrique, speaking through don Enrique, they would arrive at an agreement with the owners. He drank coffee in silence, motionless, trying not to make a sound, as if he had found a posture which he could maintain for centuries without moving. The noise of the land spread out around him as if someone were watching his back from the void. In the intensity of the night the moon ascended slowly, no longer part of a system of stars, but of a profundity which would sink more deeply in the center of the heavens, burning the stars with its whiteness, and never fall below the horizon. Thoughts, voices, memories, passed through his mind, and behind it all was a nostalgia, a voice expressing a question, wordlessly. He felt unprotected as if every door had opened and he remained exposed to his destinies. The bonfire burned on next to him, rooted in the noise of the earth, of crickets, of stars. The heavy weight of the moon went on falling like frozen water, on the rocks, on the earth, on his hands, like a revealing thought or an admonition. He closed his eyes a minute; then he opened them and looked at the fire, the earth, the boy sleeping. He closed his eyes again and it was as if another campfire, of days or of dawns bathed him with their intimate and profound breath. Suddenly he seemed to be on the point of understanding something that encompassed his entire life, that swept him along dizzily, a flaming horse that carried him to hear a veil ripped aside by a torrent; he felt himself on the point of comprehending something forever, but it was only a breeze on his lips or in his ears, above his disordered thought. He wanted to keep his eyes closed, listening to the fire, hearing his own breathing. He opened his eyes near morning, with the cup of coffee still between his hands, squeezing it tensely, his hands clinging to it as if it were a stone that was sheltering, aiding him. He sat with his eyes open, without feeling sleepy; he felt that in sleeping he hadn't lost the consciousness he'd enjoyed during the night. He changed position. He looked at the wrinkled, dusty clothes in which he had slept on the ground, in which he had awakened as if he hadn't slept for a single moment or it didn't matter. An emptiness rose in his stomach, a hand that pressed from within. *My God,* Alfredo thought, *I'm feeling it again. No, not now.* He thought about the cattle land around the vein, but now the bitterness, as if his soul had been clean and a thought had stained it, had wounded it with a cold caress. He lit some branches in the embers of the fire and heated coffee and something to eat. He thought about Parral, but with feelings that were strange and ambivalent and which did not go away with the coffee, with the fatigue, with the day, because it was a part of his soul that he had never felt nor known, lacerated like a void, creating a feeling of incompleteness, of limited existence. Stirring the fire again, he looked at the boy a few feet away, restless, eyelids moving, the muscles of his face contracted. Alfredo called him in a low voice, taking sips of his coffee. He called him again. The boy sat up and without talking looked at the food on the fire. The boy took a fistful of dirt and rubbed it in his hand, and then let it run smoothly through his fingers. He raised his eyes to Alfredo. A blue clarity grew on the horizon, and the clouds in the east began to redden as if time had stopped in another daybreak, in a vanished dawn. The boy served himself some coffee, but he didn't want to eat. Alfredo bit into a piece of dried meat and bread. The food felt like a part of himself, like another place in his life. He watched day break, the advance of the incandescent acorn of the sun across the hills, like a birth or the hardest cry, forsaken in the expanse in which light must fall during many hours in many places. He and the boy secured their samples from the deposit, collected all their things, and prepared the animals. It took them an hour to get on the road. Everything was dry, and the sun began to move upwards. The summer produced a continuous noise, self-enclosed. Soon the sun would be insupportable. Much later, many thoughts later, Alfredo found himself in the same rut, opening days like rocks without walls, without nuclei. It made him tireless, impervious to fatigue or to personal discomfort.

Before midday they arrived at Minas Nuevas. The destroyed avenues, the remains of walls and streets, reached out to them from every direction like an old silken neckerchief paralyzed by time, like a dry root that has been pulled to the surface for the sun to devour. The suffocating heat sounded in the earth with a murmur of cicadas. They went through the plaza, past the ruins of City Hall. They dismounted in front of the shop. Old Andrés approached them. Alfredo was euphoric; he laughed, he pounded the counter, saying Minas Nuevas was going to live again. The noise of summer increased inside the shop in the peaceful, heavy air where the owner dampened the earthen floor with a bucket of water. They drank warm beers. The boy left the shop, going toward the animals. Old Andrés went out to keep him company. Alfredo saw him and took a few steps, shouting when he left the shop that the old man should leave the boy alone and not bother him.

"He doesn't know anything about mines. Ask me, old man," they say he shouted again.

The Present
VI

Alfredo heard the change in his blood, a strange awakening in the veins. Life drew further away, more distant, as if some arteries were being opened, cleared out. It was a hot and heavy blow. In his chest it felt as if another hand were trying to find his own to clasp it, as if a remote and heated explosion were endeavoring to come forth, or to remain there to verify its walls in order that they might not fall, giving notice that *it* had come. He raised his eyes toward the noise, toward the shouts. Then he sought the inexpressive glance of the boy, the sweaty forehead, the mouth half open with fatigue.

"They think they can kill us," said Alfredo. "They think they can kill us."

The boy looked at him without understanding. Little by little he became aware of his sweaty hands, his heavy forehead, the bitterness in his mouth. Little by little the boy began to understand that he felt fear, a fear without reason, without origin. A fear only of the body, without consciousness, like being hungry, like waking up in surprise at midnight without recognizing anyone, without accepting anyone. Fleetingly he remembered the morning and Alfredo's waking him; for a moment he didn't know if it was today or months, years ago. His breathing was painful, throbbing tensely with a single thought. He felt its coldness and heard himself breathe. He made them out at a table near the entrance. The three were armed. The boy felt the sweat on his back, in the palms of his hands. He turned to Alfredo. He drank a cup of mezcal, almost without noticing the flavor. They came from the sierra of Guadalupe y Calvo. The man with the bolo tie had lectured Alfredo for having insulted them in El Suchiate, but all the boy remembered was that he had drunk with them. Alfredo no longer noticed. He saw the cigarettes, the matches, the cups, his hands like two stones thrown on the damp wood, waiting. He took a sip of beer. Then, softly, he felt a warm hand at the back of his neck, its slow touch oppressing him, moving his hair, passing along a neck dampened with sweat; he was held there, without violence. He moved his head from one side to the other, but then he knew that he hadn't moved it, that it was impossible. He raised one of his hands through the thickness of the cries, the smoke, the heat, and placed it on his neck, but he felt only his hair, only his sweat, the drops falling down his shoulders, down his back. He saw his hand on the table, motionless, the same as the other, and he didn't know which hand had moved. *I'm tired,* he thought. *It's something inside me, that's all.* He took the dampened bottle with the label about to come loose from the glass and brought it to his mouth. He tasted the bitterness of the beer, its foam, its acridness. *It's inside me,* he said to himself. He heard more noise, more shouts, more voices; on raising his hand, on searching his neck, he seemed to penetrate the foam in the air and to carry it full of noises, shouts, deafening music, heat, and bring it to his head, pile it on his head. *It's inside of me,* he told himself again, *and that's all there is to it.*

"Sons of bitches," he said in a loud voice, looking at their peaceful forms in the distance. "Sons of bitches."

During his final years in Parral before leaving for Minas Nuevas, the streets, the men, the transport trucks had risen in his memory or in his days like a seasickness, a fatigue, a distrust that anything was worth the trouble or made any sense. He never did understand that the breath of the years could decay in him, ending his strength, his life, as it had begun to do in the rest of us. But that passivity, that exhaustion which he had lived before leaving for Minas Nuevas, had surrounded him like a warning. While he was driving transport trucks full of cement, cattle, or wood, he told all of us how impossible it was, how useless; it would last three, four, six months and he would quit the job because the nights, the weeks, the days on the road left him increasingly empty. The alternative: to continue in the house Irene had inherited from her father, reaping the benefit of the domestic animals she had purchased and the wages his son-in-law brought home; living this way, for months. But the summer calm, the noise of the heat or of the river, the rains of the final year before leaving for Minas Nuevas, the humidity and the excessive heat, entered his lungs perversely, filling him with the odor of wildflowers, of rain and the river, of trash that was dragged through Parral when it rained and the river level rose, causing everything to smell of stale water, of dead animals; that breath, that being tied to the earth while feeling it was also his, that it was good to remain here forever.

I'll get up, thought Alfredo, breathing hard but also with difficulty. He sought out his cigarettes behind the cups. The wrapper was damp. He took one between his fingers and closed his hand. He got out his matches and struck a light. He saw the coal in the cigarette; he saw it come alive as he smoked. Meanwhile his attention turned to the noise of the brothel, to the shouts and the heat. He tried to speak to the boy, but he heard himself say no, it wasn't that. *It's the heat,* he thought. *I ought to get up for a moment.* Then he felt himself laugh, he didn't know why; he felt the laughter in his chest, in his hands, begin to yield a burning pleasure; and he tried to contain it, but it kept coming out. Alfredo was aware of a weight from within, a little light of anguish or of repentance that came out past his tongue and which he tried to spit, to strangle with the smoke of the cigarette. *It's useless,* he thought. *There are many things now.* He took the package of cigarettes again and shook out another in order to light it against the tip of the previous one. He remained silent and turned to look at the brothel. The warm hand continued at the nape of his neck, softly, without violence. He laughed again, the pleasure burning him inside, and he tried to control it, but the laughter shook him; he didn't know how, but he realized he was laughing at himself because he had spent so much time living this way, now that he had found the vein somewhere else. And he told himself that it was a test. *It's so I can change,* he thought, *so I can show myself I'm right, that I'll do what I have to.* Then he felt again how the little light came out to his tongue and remained lit there. He realized some time had passed since he'd taken a drink, and he looked around the table, but all he saw was the boy's glass. He ordered more beer, more, enough for his thirst, for his need. Alfredo understood that he was happy or something like it; or he thought he was well, that he liked being this way, that he liked this moment, that he was happy in a body full of years, of noises, of voices, of people, full of their music and cries, as if he were falling within himself, among many things; he believed he understood something, saw something else finally, understood much without words, together with memories, years, voices, places, groups of men who had become confused within him like the noise of the brothel and the heat; and he asked himself why he hadn't realized it before. *Why wasn't I this way before?* Alfredo asked himself. *Why wasn't I this way before?* he thought, and without trying to speak felt it all, within and outside himself: the tables, the light above the people, above the noise.

During those weeks the nights turned cool in the shadow of the hills; the air like a large black crystal, glittering with stars and humidity, was like a presence in the coolness of the night. There was a euphoria as if the rain were a multiple sensation which afterwards remained in the air, uneasy, charged with desire. We walked with some of his trucking friends; we stopped in the plaza or went in somewhere for a drink. Sometimes he waited for me in the afternoon at the school. When we walked, he often talked to excess, understanding that he spoke of useless things, of impossible worn-out mines. But a fury gripped him day after day, hour after hour, to unite himself with the one mine, with the ultimate mine. The week that he told me of his plans to journey to Minas Nuevas it rained continuously. The rain fell with an intensity that came from beyond the hills or the bursting clouds, that came from an ungovernable sun; and the horizon became stained with a different light as the torment moaned over Parral, with fury, as if the evening were a hybrid that embraced itself in the presence of many metals and many lovers, now fallen in the swollen river, its currents bellowing like a bloodless piece of the afternoon and shouting beneath a sun which descended further than the rain, further than the hills, further than the hardness of a world or of an aged god, abandoned to minerals, to the charge of dynamite which opens the necessity of the mine in the body, in the blood, in the life that rains over men.

The Present
VII

Yes, that's the way it was. The boy was afraid; everyone mentioned it later. He wanted to lift Alfredo up, but his arms felt tense, his legs and hands hot, and suddenly he realized he was surrounded by people, many voices, shouts, rattling glasses. He let him down. Alfredo smiled confusedly, from drunkenness or scorn. He looked with a new intensity at his dirty hands on the table, as if the necessity of life were terrible. Vaguely he remembered the voice of Andrés in the shadow of the shop. Perhaps the old man already knew the place also. Where else could a mine be but in its place? He remembered the morning with nostalgia, as if hours had not passed since then, but years. *My God,* he thought, *something that is there for no reason, in order that one can return to see who calls him, and there never is anyone. My God, there's never anybody.* Alfredo didn't hear what the boy repeated. He had no desire to speak. He saw him rubbing his sweaty hands on his clothes, eyes sunken. He thought again about the owners of the land. If they already knew about it, they wouldn't be long in looking for them; what they needed had to happen, to arrive at an agreement without wasting more days. But don Enrique wasn't there. Everything had been a fantasy, an error. *My God,* he thought, *all that work again, all that work.* The boy tried to convince him to leave with the patrol of soldiers so they could save themselves from the men from Guadalupe y Calvo. Alfredo heard the noise that seemed like a distant echo of his life, of his mind. He remembered the morning again, the trucks and the automobiles that passed near them on the road, sinking the noise of their motors in his heart, in the corners of his brain, awakening his life, the memories of the roads in the trailer, in the trucks from the mines when the sound of the motor was the voice of a human treading the land, caressing it at each wheel rut as though he were a crazed lover in an act of love that fled like the thought, but impregnated the earth. Then the rush of owning a house, of having children, *still with this other fully present,* he had told me at Robles's table, *this hurry during which everything can be lost, Armando, like when I'm going to sleep and I close my eyes and feel I'm falling into a void and the dizziness makes me open them and then I don't know what happens.* He brought his hand to his chest and studied his fist carefully and thought *that's the way it is; that's the fist that's calling me,* and he felt the heat, the sweat; *that's the way it is, like knocking at a door, as if entry were won and the doors open, and nevertheless it knocks.* His mouth felt dry, bitter, and he wanted to spit. Each mine, each year came with the loss of many things that bound him to this world, with the loss of will or hope which blended together and that now were unavoidably separate again. He seemed to recover another life, a life which suddenly calls from behind and when one turns to see is only an echo, a distorted glance full of wind or blood trying to look at us, to give us something finally that never mattered and will not matter to us again. Without taking his eyes from him, Alfredo stopped noticing the boy. He tried to concentrate and focus his attention, to hear only the knock of blood in his chest, to limit his awareness to that sound and the sweat that slid along the fine hairs of his body, down his back, through his armpits as if the sap had begun to spill from a tree because of too much summer.

As if in the vein of time destiny blossomed and the punishment was to have all doors open without being able to close off what we seek across the days, because it would be necessary to close them all step by step until it was as though they never existed. That is not destiny, but a memory that crosses centuries and worlds in order to exploit us and has no voice in our already-corrupted chests. As if the mine burnt in the soul, in a memory that no one understands and the body finds out is thus: that the mine is more than destiny, because destiny doesn't respond, it exhorts, exploits; because man reduces the mine to pieces as he is reduced to sweat or thoughts, and he responds as destiny can't, although destiny hovers near and lives in him, stuck to him, exploiting his flesh and his blood and his thoughts in order to be.

(It's the same, remember, Armando? he told me when he was at Robles's table. Clearly it's the same. All this returns because I sit here, without getting up. Each time I left on a trip, each time I went with my father to the mining camps, I felt it. Remember, Armando . . .? I would like to see those afternoons, to look at the garden again, at the women who crossed it . . . No, it's not the calm, no. What does it matter if it's the boy who accompanies me, Armando? Once I thought everything would be quicker. Or easier, maybe, I don't really know. Money has gone by like a river

that dampens some men and not others. Now everything is difficult. I can't pull anything out of that river to put in the pot. It's that no one goes further afield than he has to, no one except me. I don't want life to cover my ears, to tie my hands, you understand? To overcome everything, bad luck, fatigue, yourself the last resort. To persist by strength of will over all that I have lived. To overcome the death of my child, the aging of Irene, the shrinking of the world, of my house. To be strong in spite of myself, Armando. To show myself that I can do it although my head bursts with all the resentments, although this fatigue makes me impatient, returning like the water which rots the earth in the mines. Do you understand, Armando? Tell me, do you remember what I told you? Only that, only my body here, my fifty-seven years here, the pieces of my family, my bits of rest; only my will to help me now, to pit all that I have lived against this moment that leaps like a fistful of hunger that arrives at the table quickly, but always late.)

Alfredo took the boy by the arm. He lifted him from the table and dragged him toward the door, knocking over a chair. The boy looked at several faces, but none turned to look at him, as if he could have passed hours or days abandoned on the floor of the brothel, covered by his fatigue.

"Let's go, Alfredo. Now, let's go . . ." mumbled the boy.

The burning sweat from his forehead entered his eyes, but he confused it with something that burned even more, with his hand that rubbed at his eyelids or something even deeper. They passed near the table with the men from Guadalupe y Calvo; only the old man turned to look at Alfredo. Covered with sweat and fatigue, the boy looked at them. Alfredo stopped in the doorway. All at once the boy felt that coolness of the night, of a sky that opened suddenly above them like two hands that separate and allow the face to be seen by the distant lights of the houses. A few steps away two men were talking, drunk. They didn't turn to look, not even when Alfredo spat near them. At times the boy felt that Alfredo's words were blows that went into his arm or his chest and began to disintegrate there, to fill him with dirt from within, to mix with his blood the way mud is formed. Alfredo moved closer to speak to him, but without letting him go. The boy's hands were damp with sweat; he rubbed his clothes with his free hand, but on the other the sweat increased as if he had squeezed a sponge full of ice water. Afterwards Alfredo hit him, insulted him, determined to run him out of there, and the boy noticed that for some time the two men had stopped talking and watched him with reddened eyes, inoffensively. A blow stung his face as if someone had thrown a fistful of heat to burn him. Behind him was Parral, its silent houses, the sleep that was lost in the hot night while the pain continued. He turned toward the two men, saw their hats tipped back, their reddened eyes appearing idiotic and without menace. They only seemed to be intent on something that was happening near them, thoughtless, unquestioning. But they looked him in the eyes as if they had found a deep road there and understood it well. He turned toward Alfredo, who was observing the night, the dark and quiet bushes in the river bed. Alfredo spat. He went into the brothel. At his back the boy heard the men return to their discussion without any sign of being otherwise preoccupied. He remained motionless, watching Alfredo move forward between the tables. Remaining with him was a vague discomfort which came with living, from being able to feel.

"Let's go, Alfredo, I tell you," he murmured, still in a low voice. "Let's go, understand, let's go."

Something reached the boy's ears from a great distance; it was a message or a restlessness, something which had been lost for a long time. He thought suddenly of the nights when, as a boy, he made his way home through the ruins of Talamantes de Arriba, through a dust which grew thicker, heavier, while he ran without knowing if he was fleeing something evil or a blessing, until he arrived at his house, when he looked again to see if someone still came after him over the land, in the noise of the night.

He didn't know how much time went by before he left. It was already late, past twelve o'clock or maybe one, because at that moment the troop of soldiers entered the brothel. The moon burst silently, slowly in the sky. He stopped in the middle of the river bed, but felt an overpowering desire to go on. The voices and the music had grown more distant. He arrived at the other shore. Something sunk within himself, as a very slender, dusty straw will sink in a glass of water, releasing all its dust. On starting down the street, he stopped again. He wished to return, to fight next to Alfredo. Or to speak with the soldiers. Far away he could see the whorehouses. He noted that he was changing, that something new was taking shape in him which left him exposed. He looked for a cigarette, but he had left them on the table. At that moment he felt his desire to smoke was like his desire to understand life. He noticed that his hands were no longer sweating. He opened them in front of his face and looked at them; in a short while the sweat broke forth. He stopped further along. Then he walked with a different sense of weight in his legs, as if he were learning to walk or had already forgotten how.

Some dogs rose in his path; in the doorways and in all the nearby streets they began to bark. He turned to the left, toward the road leading to the bridge. His thoughts oppressed him. He arrived at the level land of Botello's orchard. Then he noticed he had forgotten the noise of the crickets, of the night. Soon the need for Ana grew in him; his memory gave her a precise shape. Moments passed in which he could hear the voice of Alfredo in his mind, accompanied by a doubt as to Alfredo's state of fatigue, his health. He crossed the railroad bridge and came to the rocky part of the street. He turned to look involuntarily at the houses where there was light. He thought that the death of a man is part of being a man, and he began to talk out loud. When the earth of the hill came under his feet, another world seemed to open indistinctly within him. Using his soul as a measure, he counted the brief moments of his final steps. Arriving at Ana's house, he felt overwhelmed from within by a sadness of something half perceived, and he stopped, shaken, before calling out to her, listening to the loneliness of the night. In the distance he saw the scattered lights of the city, like the eyes of an animal breathing. He called Ana wordlessly from his silence, and remained agitated, trembling, as if the woman of love, or the unknown woman of love, always rouses fear in a man because of something unknown and very terrible that he begins to know, or as if something were very near, beyond the darkness of what he has lived or of what one has possessed, as one would tremble before a grace, before a blessing or a repentance. He slept the next day until noon. It was there they found him in the afternoon, with the woman.

The Present
VIII

Ana approaches the edge of the bed. She places her feet on the earthen floor, which is still slightly warm. She is aware of the warmth of the bed, the odor of rumpled sheets. She lights the oil stove and places a pot of water with orange leaves on its surface to heat. She goes over to the window. She feels her breasts, slightly upbraided by caresses, her aching thighs. She lifts the curtain and looks at the afternoon through the glass. A boy with a flock of goats comes slowly toward her from the distance. She feels the steam from the boiling water on her face and smells the fragrant odor of the orange leaves. Since he arrived in the night, the closed house has retained its heat. The boy keeps talking about Alfredo, telling her again about what they did. He goes on and on, like all the men she has been with.

Ana leaves the cups next to the stove. She turns off the oven. Everything is quiet, filled with the warmth of sleep, of permanence, as if everything were on the point of going to sleep or about to create life anew. She places the dirty cups in the bucket of water. She is aware of perspiration all over her body. She returns to the window and opens the curtain. She studies the boy and the flock of approaching goats. She thinks in terms of weariness, of sweat, of the boring pace of this country. She thinks that the boy and the goats can't imagine a nude woman like her looking at them. She thinks about Alfredo Montenegro, but can't really remember him. She only knows that his presence bothered her when he spoke, when he tried to be funny. The whitest cloud is suspended over the hill. She leans back and feels the coolness of the wall. She hears the muffled laughter of the goatherd, indistinct as he passes near the window, playing with the goats, which move as one in rapid, nervous rushes. She hears their many bleats as they trot past the house. When they disappear, she contemplates the dust that they raised. She continues trying to hear the noise of the goats or the echo of the boy's shouts, but there is more silence, as if something has been torn out of the afternoon and a hole remained. She looks at the hill, at the quiet afternoon, without thinking anything, bathed by the heat.

On hearing them, Ana sits up. She feels the warm bed under her, under the boy. In her something awakes that is vaguely familiar, as if all her desires took flight and she is totally exposed again. The horses stop; their hooves paw the earth. Ana feels the warm hand of the boy on her back, the sweat, the heat. She holds her breath. Through the window she sees the afternoon light. One of the horses neighs.

"Jesús González!" they shout outside the house. "Jesús González!" they cry even louder.

Naked himself, the boy sees the breasts and thighs of

Ana in the darkness. He feels a visceral desire bred of the accumulated months. Ana separates herself as far as possible and looks for a dress. They call him again, but the bed is steeped in Ana's odor; he wishes the time would go more slowly, that nothing would ever change. He puts on pants only. He wants to look at her, to remain thus, motionless next to her. Outside, the horses strike their hooves on the ground, neighing. The shouting resumes. The boy leans against the door. He opens it. *(Because I knew what was going on, Ana. I understood. Today we would see a friend of his to reach an agreement. Because we were going to work the mine, you see. It could be done, yes. Alfredo was sure. I can do it, Ana. I believe I can do it also. Because Alfredo said that if you've only worked as a peon for ASARCO, or some other company, you don't know what a mine is because you have the soul of your work, the soul of a peon. But now no one wanted to go with him to Minas Nuevas, only me, understand? And I could take or leave the work, although I felt obligated, Ana. But I worked. I did a lot of work, and it made me feel important, understand? Not only Alfredo. But me too, yes, me too . . .)*

He opens the door and is struck by the intense brightness of the afternoon. One man holds the horses and the other three are waiting. The air is clean; the afternoon is clean. The hills seem to rise up in the liberty of their vastness. His bare feet move on the earth and surprise him with their recognition of the warm dust, the sun, the heat, as if they hadn't done it for years. From the window Ana looks at the boy's naked back; with a quiet that sinks in her like desperation, she runs down it to his bare feet, as if the afternoon has taken that means to penetrate her, wounding like a dagger in the hand, a hot blow.

"We wanted to see you two together, but now that's impossible," one of them says. "You can imagine what happened to Alfredo . . . We thought you were his friend. You should have stayed to defend him."

The boy feels the cleanliness of the afternoon in his body, of the summer. As he stands there in the dust, he remembers many days, many moments of his life. He looks at the hill full of underbrush and drought. On turning, he sees Ana in the window and immediately feels love for her. His mouth is dry. He wants to drink a little water while he is here. He looks at some houses scattered on a nearby hill. The entire horizon is open, clean.

"We've come on behalf of the Chávezes. That land wasn't yours, and the mine isn't going to be either."

(It was surprising, Ana, like realizing that something from years past is next to you and you don't see it till the last moment. I loved you so much in that moment, Ana, you can't imagine it. It was as if there were many doors in life, or inside you. Alfredo says that's destiny, that there destiny lies. That he had chosen it, but I hadn't.)

"I don't give a damn," says the boy. "I do what I have to."

He hears the bleating of the goats in the distance, the return of the cattle, the cries of the youths who guide them as they enter the village. He thinks about his own village, Talamantes de Arriba, and about the tepid current of the river. Afterwards he thinks about Amelia. But he understands there is little time for words, little time to hope and to complete the things that make up his flesh: the afternoon, this twisting road that surges toward him like the feeling, together with the noise of Parral, an urgency that is sadness or bravery. Never has he been so clear of head as now, conscious of each part of his body, of each instant.

"Yes, that's the reason we came."

He feels the clearest light of the afternoon, of the open sky, sunk infinitely into himself, like a distant sound or an enormous face. *"So you're a miner, kid," Alfredo said to him the afternoon they met. "You call yourself a miner." One night in the house of Antonio's brother, who had worked on his shift in the mine, he heard his future boss discussed. They didn't know much about Alfredo except that he was looking for a mine. It was easy to imagine nights in the sierra, alone, but that was all. Also he entertained a very distant, very profound idea that maybe he could do it. Alfredo was securing the load of wood on the trailer. "It's not a matter of a few days, kid," Alfredo said to him that afternoon. "I've been doing this for several years. But it's not a matter of days, no." And the afternoon was beautiful. Yes, the afternoon was beautiful, the boy remembered, standing silently beside the trailer, waiting for Alfredo to hire him.)* He looks at the shining afternoon and fleetingly remembers Villa Escobedo. It seems there are many skies in this one sky, many places in that place, and time is like the black silver or like silence, and in the middle of it all he feels alone, as if a calm bordering on menace hung in the sky. Ana appears and leans in the angle of the doorway. Once more the same love that he felt on arriving stirs in his chest, a physical love that shakes him as if the whole world consisted of that body; he feels a bright grief spreading through him at not being able to embrace her, at not being able to return to her for centuries. Fleetingly, Alfredo is a memory in the night, where he sits holding a cup of coffee beside the fire. Two of the men move their hands toward their pistols and unholster them. Within his body he feels a sudden vomit that tears at the roots of his soul and a pain so enormous he can't tell what it is, only the hot contact of something moving with a burning velocity, a maddened blow he tries vainly to ward off with his hands. Suddenly the afternoon turns slow, extremely slow, as if he has not breathed for an eternity, while a flower is torn to pieces inside him, exposing vulnerable petals that no one can hear. Like a day gone crazy, he hears Ana rush from the house, crying to a day that begins in the earth and tries to move, trembles, its stones clamoring hoarsely beneath his feet. The men fire. The boy succeeds in hearing the shots, like explosions in the hills, shouts from the earth and the afternoon, as if suddenly the mine opened all its avenues and the rocks and the metal surged forth inside him, as if all his life had been lived equal to Alfredo's, and a nostalgia invades him, a blossoming of bright flowers so numerous they appear like birds flying out of his life, carrying a fragrance of love, memories that suffocate him, falling with a sweet weight like the sun; and he wants to see it all, but the men have grown very far away, muffled. He wants to throw off the weight that he feels on top of him, that he senses inside, and he vomits repentance as distance rises up and with it the desire to shout, to cry; and confusedly he feels Ana's presence beside him as he tries to spit out something that fills his mouth, the silence of exploding words; and he feels distant tears, weariness weighing him down, and there are pieces of something in his mouth that taste of calm.

Carlos Montemayor was born in 1947 in Parral in the State of Chihuahua, Mexico. His efforts at fiction have won one prize after another, beginning with the Premio Xavier Villaurrutia for his first collection of stories, *Llaves de Urgell,* and ending with the Premio Colima for his latest novel, *Guerra en el Paraíso.* His most recent story, "Operativo en el trópico," was awarded the Premio Juan Rulfo de Radio Francia Internacional, and *Gambusino* won *El Nacional*'s 50th Anniversary Novel Contest. He currently resides in Mexico City.

TURN PAGE FOR DATE DUE SLIP